Beauty and Love

Texts and Translations

The MLA series Texts and Translations was founded in 1991 to provide students and faculty members with important texts and high-quality translations that otherwise would not be available at an affordable price. The books in the series are aimed at students in upper-level undergraduate and graduate courses—in national literatures in languages other than English, comparative literature, literature in translation, ethnic studies, area studies, and women's studies.

For a complete listing of titles, see the last pages of this book.

ŞEYH GALIP

Beauty and Love

Translated from the Ottoman Turkish
with an introduction and key by
Victoria Rowe Holbrook

The Modern Language Association of America
New York   2005

Printed in the United States of America

MLA and the MODERN LANGUAGE ASSOCIATION are trademarks owned by the
Modern Language Association of America. For information about obtaining permission
to reprint material from MLA book publications, send your request
by mail (see address below) or e-mail (permissions@mla.org).

Library of Congress Cataloging-in-Publication Data
Şeyh Galip, 1757 (or 1758)–1799.
[Hüsn ü Aşk. English]
Beauty and Love / Seyh Galip ; translated from the Ottoman Turkish
with an introduction and key by Victoria Rowe Holbrook.
pages cm.
ISBN 978-0-87352-934-1
I. Holbrook, Victoria Rowe, 1952– . II. Title.
PL248.S387A28 2005
894'.3512—dc22   2005050132

Texts and Translations 17
ISSN 1079-2538

Cover illustration: couplet 55 of Galip's work
("The heart's speck of black light opened out wide / Concealing
the journey by night inside"), drawn by Ali Alparslan, professor
of calligraphy at Mimar Sinan University

Third printing 2016

Published by The Modern Language Association of America
85 Broad Street, suite 500, New York, New York 10004-2434
www.mla.org

This translation is dedicated to
Mary Forrester

TABLE OF CONTENTS

INTRODUCTION

Şeyh Galip's Ottoman Turkish romance *Beauty and Love* seems a familiar tale.[1] The story of a hero who matures through trials to win his beloved is universal. That the hero is named Love and the heroine Beauty seems a recognizable allegory. But that is only partly true.

The writing of Turkish romances in rhyming couplets had become rare in Galip's time. *Beauty and Love*, finished in 1783, is short for the genre. The classics often ran to five or six thousand verses. Galip, characteristically boastful, made it clear that he considered his contemporaries mediocre and his work to be in the line of the greatest romances of his predecessors, whom he named. In retrospect his contemporaries have been judged undistinguished, and *Beauty and Love* is widely considered the greatest work of Ottoman literature. In fact Galip handled his tradition in such a way that his work is both an innovation and a summary of it. Integrated into the work are many of the tradition's major themes and debates *and their historical development*. In this way *Beauty and Love* can be the best introduction to Islamic literature there is. The work is short, because it is highly condensed—he referred to stories, themes, and arguments his readers knew and didn't need recounted, only indicated. That this is done with a sense of humor, often wild humor, and virtuoso fun is another pleasure. The work is an extraordinary mixture of wide-eyed fairy tale and formidable erudition.

Galip was born into an Istanbul family that for generations had been closely tied to the Mevlevi dervish order, named after Mevlana Jelaleddin Rumi, the famous mystic poet, presently the best-selling poet in the United States. To call Rumi a mystic does not evoke the breadth of work typical of the Muslim sages known for writing many volumes in verse of ethical teachings based on a distinctive ontology expounded in tales. That ontology was not named; rather it was generally assumed, so much so that it could almost be called the medieval Muslim worldview, but not quite. It still remains a way of seeing things, and it was never so unquestioned that it could be said to characterize the age or the religion. It was elaborated early in Muslim history and was always disputed, even as it became more widely accepted as time went on, especially in the Ottoman Empire. In Ottoman times the ontology was associated with Ibn Arabi and his Turkish school and sometimes referred to by the term *vahdet-i vücut* ("the unity of being"). It is the ontology of the unity of being that accounts for much of what would not, to a reader untutored in the tradition, be familiar about *Beauty and Love*.

Galip wrote in the Turkish tradition combining the teachings of Rumi and Ibn Arabi, or perhaps more accurately in many cases, interpreting Rumi through Ibn Arabi. Rumi was born in Balkh, settled in Anatolia with his family as a youth, wrote in Persian, and died in 1272. Ibn Arabi was born in Murcia, traveled widely throughout much of his life, wrote in Arabic, and died in Damascus in 1240. Together they were the most powerful influences on Ottoman religion and literature; Ottoman thought became organized in ways Ibn Arabi initiated, much as Christian thought remained for centuries organized in ways Saint Thomas Aquinas articulated. Galip was born in Istanbul in 1758, appointed şeyh of the Galata Mevlevi House in Istanbul in 1790, and died in 1799. To say *Beauty and Love* was written in that tradition means specific things for interpretation of the work, and Galip made these criteria explicit by way of his allusions.

Love and Beauty are allegorical figures, but not just allegories of qualities; they represent God's qualities. They are not exactly allegories of God's qualities because every thing in the world is made of God's qualities and represents them in something like an allegorical manner. As the Koran tells us, every thing in the world is a sign of God. So an allegory of God's qualities can in a sense be a description of reality. Love's journey is that of all humanity through stages of being, each stage having its proper realm. Love meets a demon who wants to eat him, a witch who wants to marry him, and an illusory Chinese princess who traps him in her Fortress of Forms. There is an allegory of the composite soul as understood by medievals here: the vegetal soul, whose functions are assimilation and growth; the animal soul, characterized by lust and anger; and the rational soul, whose weakness is that it can be duped by logic. The Chinese princess looks exactly like Beauty, and therefore it is rational for Love to believe she is Beauty, but according to the tradition, truth, ultimate reality, is beyond intellect in the realm of spirit, with which the subtler levels of the soul, itself the result of a mixture of spirit and body, overlap. This sort of allegory—a journey through the microcosm—was quite popular from the twelfth century on, but not as part of a romance. Some of these allegories included a full journey through the body, soul, and spirit, while Galip, in characteristically shorthand manner, focused on the journey through the soul. Its extension, a journey through the macrocosm, was also not part of romance tradition and is found in *Beauty and Love*.

This is partly what I mean when I say Galip integrated the historical development of his tradition into *Beauty and Love*. By situating these elements within his work, Galip picked up a trend in romance tradition where it had been left in the sixteenth century by Fuzuli, whom he considered the last great romance writer in Turkish. That trend was the allegorization of the old love tales. But in eighteenth-century Istanbul, allegorization had long since come to be understood in light of the unity-of-being ontology. In Fuzuli's *Leyla and Majnun* love between a man and a woman is a likeness of real love, that is, between humankind and God; Fuzuli's lovers are never united because the real ending of the story is not their union. Galip's lovers are united in the end because we are always already in the real—a novel conclusion for the romance genre. Through references and allusions Galip calls up the older love tales and the reader's expectations of them, all the while superimposing an interpretation in harmony with later Ottoman philosophical development that prepared the way for a new conclusion.

The macrocosmic counterpart to the composite soul is the composite universe, with its sensory realm in layers of earth, water, fire, air, the heavenly spheres, and variously named realms beyond. The demon lives deep in the earth at the bottom of a pit; the witch, between an icy winterscape and a sea of fire; the Fortress of Forms is described in ethereal terms. Love does not follow the path of a journey through the seven heavens, a component common to many works, most famously Attar's *Conference of the Birds*. Galip did insert a lighthearted treatment of this much-worked theme in a prefatory chapter on the Miraj, the Prophet's spiritual journey; but Love moves directly on to the beyond, as had become customary in later allegories of the dervish path. It is just beyond the seven heavens that the realm of imagination is usually considered to be located. The Fortress of Forms is that place. After that, Love moves on to a realm of abstraction, the spiritual realm where things subsist without form.

Most broadly characterized, the macrocosm has sensory, imaginal, and spiritual realms of many levels, corresponding to the body, soul, and spirit of the human microcosm. All things originate in God, and while they "descend" to embodied existence in the sensory realm, they continue to subsist in the divine realm in a spiritual state. Imagination is a faculty of the soul, its contents, and also the intermediate macrocosmic level that is the domain of the soul, where things subsist as forms without matter, similar to images, in the imaginal state. In this understanding, the contents of the mind are not manufactured by the mind; rather, they are the soul's apperception of forms in the imaginal state, and that apperception depends on the condition of one's soul. The faculties of the soul are located in the heart, which is often likened to a mirror. Worship of God "polishes" that mirror. Thus the images in our minds differ in part according to the clarity of our hearts.

The life of all things begins in the spiritual, acquires form, and proceeds to material existence. That part of the journey is called the arc of descent or outward track. All things return to God, voluntarily or involuntarily. On the journey back, called the arc of ascent or inward track, one returns through the intermediary realm of imagination, where this time one loses material form. In bodily death it is in this imaginal state that one waits in the grave for the resurrection. But it is possible, as the prophet Muhammad said, to "die before you die," called a voluntary death. Allegories of the dervish path describe the inner journey of voluntary death, undertaken in order to realize the true nature of existence while one still has the chance to prepare for bodily death. In Galip's tale, voluntary death is the "alchemy" Love must find in order to be worthy of Beauty's hand. When he burns down the Fortress of Forms and emerges into a realm characterized by the Sacred Spirit, he has completed his journey through the levels of the soul to the point where it connects with spirit. He proceeds on to the Land of the Heart, which he has never really left; the difference is that the faculties of his soul are purified so that his heart can see clearly, and he sees that it is Beauty who is there, that the heart is her domain. He realizes that he has never been separate from her, that he experienced the things he did because his perception was awry. In reality Love is Beauty, as Beauty is Love.

This conclusion accords with the paradigm of love as taught by the early dervish writer Ahmad Ghazzali (died 1226; not to be confused with his more famous brother, Abu Hamid), which

Galip received through the Turkish tradition and superimposed on the romance genre, reversing the usual romance roles of male and female thereby. Beauty, the girl, is the first to fall in love with the boy. In Ghazzali's teaching, all relationships are determined by God's absolute love, objectified in the roles of lover and beloved, and beauty is the sum of perfections love possesses. God creates out of love, and so it is of course God who first takes the role of lover, while his beloved creature, turned away from God on the arc of descent, is yet unaware. At a certain point in life, human beings grow in awareness of beauty to the extent that they turn toward God, taking the role of lover on the arc of ascent. The logic of the paradigm, when applied to the romance genre, requires that the role of lover be first played by the female, something which Ibn Arabi is famous for having noticed. The two children in Galip's tale are born into a world in which all relationships are determined by love. Every member of their tribe is passionately in love[2] and interprets everything and everyone as motivated by love. The boy Love is at first unaware of Beauty, and the dawn of his awareness brings about "The Reversal of Events," a chapter that divides the work in two and marks the beginning of his journey, his arc of ascent. At first he is tremendously full of himself and his role as a heroic lover. He becomes progressively humbler as he matures through his experiences, until he realizes that his selfhood has consisted of role-playing. His companion Rivalry is no longer needed.[3] In reality he and his beloved are one and the same, made, as all creatures are, of God's love: unity of being.

The character Poetry is both the go-between of romance and the guide of dervish allegory, while also carrying associations common to the logos. But he is something else, special to Galip, which is briefly indicated in Galip's prefatory chapter in praise of God (which I discuss below) and becomes clear in the Digression on the nature of poetry just after Poetry makes his first appearance in the tale.[4] For Galip, poetry was a path to God, because it is the best form of speech (and since

God creates with speech, speech can be followed back to him); because it is imaginative—properly, imaginal, when it is the true poetry he believed in; and because, as he explains in the Digression, it is the form of speech in which poets realize the incomparability of the Koran. The two children find Poetry in the Pleasure Place of Meaning, a garden where their love becomes mutual under his influence, but as Galip characterizes him, he is everywhere. It was customary in allegories of the dervish path for the journey to begin with a meeting with a guide figure in a place outside the city. The imagery Galip uses to describe the garden suggests a level overlapping with the spiritual realm. Everything is in a state of infinite expansiveness, eternally, but does have form. It is watered by a Pool of Grace, "a sea of qualities"—referring to God's qualities, of which the world partakes—on which images constantly appear, like "the talent of a pure poet." In Turkish (as in Arabic and Persian), "meaning" is often synonymous with "spiritual" and is coupled with "form," in that all created beings have both inner meaning and outward form, a principle quite a few of Galip's images throughout the work depend on. The children have been schoolmates, learning from Professor Madness that things are not what they seem (thus the one who sees things as they really are appears mad), but it is in the Pleasure Place of Meaning that they begin to communicate. Poetry is the proper go-between for them not only because he is speech, communication, but because he works in form, in imagination, the link to the real. Then, just as the children are beginning to get along, they are separated by Lord Dazzle, the same character who unites them in the end. They must be dazzled if they are to be separated and Love to pursue Beauty (who must appear to withdraw with Modesty's intervention in order to allow for Love's development), and again dazzled if they are to be united, since the real is beyond the intellect, which is also to say beyond words. Poetry is left behind along with all the others Beauty and Love have known.

The tale is framed by prefatory chapters and an epilogue, as was customary for the romance genre. The prefatory chapters in praise of God and the Prophet were always observed, and usually a "Reason for This Composition." The others that Galip included—a Mirajiye (a treatment of the Prophet's spiritual journey, the Miraj) and the chapters in praise of Rumi and Galip's father—were optional. Because every romance began with such chapters, they tended to be repetitive and for this reason have been often overlooked—wrongly, for the choices a poet made in them tell us much about the poet's position in historically specific debates and thus how to understand the work. Here I will give some examples of this, although of course appreciation of the positions Galip took is enhanced by a knowledge of their historical context that goes beyond what I can provide here. Furthermore, these chapters, and the Digression as well, are full of references made by way of proper names or by phrases, terms, and quotations, which are italicized in my translation. In the key that follows the translation, I have explicated proper names and italicized items minimally, to the extent necessary to keep them from being an obstacle to understanding, and only as specifically relevant to *Beauty and Love*. Volumes have been written on some of these terms; in certain cases a bibliography for one item—for example, the divine names—could be longer than this introduction.

The chapter in praise of God was particularly challenging for a poet to make fresh, since not only all romances but all literary works began with praise of God. Galip's choice to keep the chapter short focuses on the inability of human beings to know God fully and therefore praise him appropriately, and places Galip in the tradition of *melamet* ("self-deprecation"). *Melamet* is a practice of keeping one's faith pure by scrupulously avoiding the courting of approval, even exposing oneself to blame, in matters of piety and especially spiritual attainment. In a society where piety is highly valued, there is an obvious temptation to show it off, with the inevitable danger of committing hypocrisy. The solution of *melamet* is to conceal piety, in various ways and to varying degrees. Galip used a certain characteristic kind of humor, making as if light of it in a way that is understood to not at all be making light of it. Praise-of-God chapters were often attempts, flowery in the extreme, to be clever. To start off by praising God for allowing speechless awe as praise of God, and to keep the chapter poor in imagery, may seem a throwaway move but is actually a self-deprecating gesture in a long tradition of *melamet*.

Melamet is associated with Ibn Arabi and in Ottoman contexts is invariably accompanied by a unity-of-being ontology. There was an Ottoman Melami dervish order, which I have called an anti-order, and there were Melami tendencies, even wings, in other orders, including the Mevlevi. Galip signaled his *melamet*-inclined Mevlevi preferences by keeping the chapter to eighteen couplets, eighteen being the traditional Mevlevi number, and by his reference in couplet 5 to the Prophet's saying, "Oh God, we have not known you as you should be known." According to Mevlevi tradition this saying was the subject of the first conversation between Rumi and his dearest friend, Shams. The point brought out in their conversation was that the Prophet, who would be expected to know God as far as God could be known, meant by saying this to show that an unquenchable thirst for knowledge, a form of spiritual poverty, is the complement of divine plenitude. The chapter ends with a brief foreshadowing of the role of poetry in union with God, beyond knowledge of him, that Galip elaborated later in the work. By giving imagination free range in poetry, one can follow the "chain" beyond intellect, dazzled. This idea resonates with Mevlevi-Melami interpretation of the doctrine of the divine names and attributes, central to unity-of-being ontology. Galip's disparaging references to certain positions in early theological debates, in couplet 8 and later in the Digression in couplet 778, and his dependence on the doctrine in the Digression indicate this characteristic interpretation. Briefly, all creation is the manifestation of God's qualities (names and attributes), which require manifestation to the extent that it is through manifestation that their potential is played out. If God

is merciful, his mercy will be manifest in action upon objects
of his mercy, and so on for the other qualities. It is thought
that people, as manifestations of divine names, can follow,
so to speak, the names back to the named. This is one of the
functions of *zikir*, the meditative chanting of the divine names.
Galip's father was also Mevlevi and, as became public after his
death from the inscription on his tombstone, Melami. Galip's
emphasis, in his chapter in praise of his father, on the spiritual
guidance he received from him, affirms these loyalties.

While the philosophical ancestry of these loyalties is ancient
and perhaps universal, they had a specific political significance
in historical context. In Galip's time the Ottoman Empire was
losing in war, and its losses were seen as the continuation of a
disastrous trend. Galip was the spiritual adviser to the sultan,
Selim III, and Selim engaged in a series of reform efforts, called
the New Order, which included the creation of a bombardier
corps along European lines. Selim appointed Galip to a special
position at the mosque he had built in the new barracks
complex of the corps, effectively making Galip spiritual adviser
to the corps. Galip wrote in support of the corps, not in *Beauty
and Love* but elsewhere, while opposition factions attacked
it, verbally and by violent sabotage, and Selim himself was
eventually assassinated. This backlash characterized itself in
terms of defense of the faith (such things as new uniforms could
be called sacrilegious), while of course there were matters of
considerable material self-interest involved; Selim's investment
of wealth in creating a new army was perceived as having been
at the old army's expense. His reforms, including land reforms
that touched the Mevlevi central administration in Konya, may
have occasioned the death threats Galip received from within
the order. Galip was barely forty when he died, probably of
tuberculosis, but there were rumors of foul play. Selim justified
his New Order in what I will call progressive religious terms,
and it was criticized in what I will call conservative religious
terms. The conservative religious argument was, broadly, that
innovation was a violation of sacred law (more precisely, of

established practice sanctioned as the result of the collective wisdom of the Muslim community). The progressive religious argument depends on an understanding of the unity of being as the source of innovation, an understanding that Galip invoked in the Digression with regard to innovation in poetry. There he argued that perpetual creation (in this interpretation the continuous re-creation of all things through the imperative of the infinite divine names[5] to manifestation) is the cause of original poetry (couplet 783). The same argument can be made in support of innovation in every sphere of life, social, political, military, and so on, and this is what Selim and Galip were doing.

Why that type of argument has not continued to be made to effect in modern Muslim societies is another story. Here we can see that the realization that one's knowledge of God can never be sufficient, coupled with an understanding of the unity of being as perpetually bringing new things into being, could be the ground for a dynamic, forward-looking attitude toward society and life in general. This dynamic view dominates the chapter in praise of the Prophet and the Mirajiye chapter. Galip focused on the relationships among God, Muhammad, and humankind. Light may be shed on the issue at hand by a proverbial saying: "The Prophet is always on the Miraj."[6] Galip's Mevlevi-Melami tradition understood the Miraj first of all as a spiritual event. Couplet 55 of the Mirajiye expressed this idea with one of the most finely constructed images in Ottoman poetry: "The heart's speck of *black light* opened out wide / Concealing the *journey by night* inside." Black light is divine light, so bright it makes the eyes grow dark. Every human heart contains a speck of it, and the whole event of the Miraj is encompassed by that speck. In this understanding, the question of how the Prophet could have been awakened one night by Gabriel, ridden a miraculous steed from Mecca to Jerusalem, led all God's prophets in prayer, ascended to heaven to meet God, and returned to Mecca to find his bed still warm is beside the point, because the event was a demonstration of an always available paradigm of humankind's true relationship with God and the inner journey. Galip's image in couplet 24 of the praise-of-the-Prophet chapter, "The door to his tent is the *space of two bows*," is the traditional explication of the proverbial saying. The "space of two bows" is a Koranic reference (see the Key), understood in this interpretation to describe the position of God and Muhammad during their meeting. A broader commentary practice interprets the phrase to mean that Muhammad came as close to God as the distance traveled by an arrow in two bow shots, or the space of two bows laid on the ground so that they are end to end. But Galip's tradition took it to mean the circle formed by two bows placed standing on end so that their strings touch and the bows are held out like two doors, a circle of unity symbolizing the true relationship between God and Muhammad and, by extension, between God and humankind. The nature of human beings is that they are microcosms of God's qualities. Each human being carries within him or her all of God's qualities, in potential. The person who actualizes all these qualities—an infinite process, since the qualities are infinite—is called a Perfect Human Being, and Muhammad was and is the paradigmatic Perfect Human Being. In this way "the Prophet is always on the Miraj."

In the progressive view nothing can be known with finality, because everything is always changing and new possibilities are the rule. It makes good sense that the Ottoman Turks, who had a highly developed sense of the anxiety of influence as relative latecomers to Islam, would have so embraced Ibn Arabi's thought as they headed west in the process of creating the mightiest of Muslim empires and with grand gestures after they conquered Istanbul,[7] while in the old world of Islam Ibn Arabi was attacked as a heretical innovator, associated with a degeneration of the Muslim community due to the Mongol invasions. It was as the self-confidence of the Ottoman and other Islamic polities worldwide began to be shaken in the seventeenth century that the conservative religious argument came to the fore sporadically in Istanbul, with Ibn Arabi taken as a target of resentment. The troubles of the late eighteenth century were seen as a continuation of the seventeenth, and Selim and Galip drew on what they saw as abiding resources of Ottoman strength.

I close by briefly taking up a different level of the work, its imagery. *Beauty and Love* also contains an archaeology of Islamicate imagery—that is, the historical stages of that imagery are visible in the work. Galip was known as the greatest Ottoman master of the Indian style, which was famous for its complex imagery and so called because it had flourished at the Turkish Mughal courts in India. In the Indian style, relations among elements in images established in the high classical poetry of the fourteenth through sixteenth century are exponentially multiplied, creating an effect a student once called psychedelic. A characteristic feature of classical Islamicate imagery is formal harmony, the comparison of objects according to their shape. A round thing—say, a face—is like the moon or the sun; or the length of a thing is highlighted by comparing it to a sword. With time certain metaphors, like moon for face, became so standard that one could refer to a beautiful person, as Galip constantly did, as "that moon." But these are extremely simple examples. Couplet 338 in the section of *Beauty and Love* where Galip compared Love as a babe in the cradle to a sword in a sheath illustrates this type of imagery paired: "Sometimes in his cradle he became peeved / A gleaming sword rattling inside its sheath." In the description of Beauty, a gloved hand and its fingers are compared to the sun and its rays: "Those hands clothed in archer's bejeweled gloves / With one single shot maimed all the sun's claws" (450). Beauty and Love are described at school: "Two bewitching eyes read spellbinding vows / School desks arched before their glances like brows" (360). Galip played with the principle of formal harmony, making light of its implausibility in such verses describing the tribe: "For cups they raised clubs with mountainous heads" (255) and "They thought a stiletto a long-stemmed glass" (257); or their wildly distracted state as they searched for a stream:

"They had in mind only liquid that flowed / A stream or a gash in flesh—who would know" (273). It is important to get a firm grasp of the principle of formal harmony, for the Indian style builds on it.

The characteristic of the Indian style is to expand upon, often distorting, formal harmony in a variety of ways. In the following couplets from the description of Beauty, the comparison of shapes is there, but as an echo. Hair and amber treasure, mole and dark-skinned man: "Her long tresses were a raw amber hoard / The mole on her cheek, its black Hindu guard" (454); heel and wine cup: "With henna that fairy painted her heel / And made reddest wine trip, stumble and reel" (456); eyes and brows and prayer niche and calligraphy: "Her black eyes and delicately curved brows / Inscribed in a prayer niche two divine vows" (481); a related comparison describing Love: "From under his cap a curly fringe fell / To God's greatest name across the moon spell" (499). In the description of the dark night of winter, the mouth of a frozen stream is compared to a grinning black man: "The cold formed with snow the mouth of a stream / The black man of night grinned showing his teeth" (1419). Love in his final stage of emaciation falls from his horse: "He fell like a shadow from Sorrel Rose / A fiery spark disengaged from its coal" (1897). A further extension is to compare a shape to an abstraction, which acquires a shape, sort of, through the comparison—as in this couplet from the chapter on Beauty's nocturnal visits to Love's room: "Without fear she roamed the darkness unheard / As if she were meaning inside a word" (577); and in this related couplet, again from Love's emaciation: "Without matter he was but a mere form / Significance rare without letter borne" (1902). Personification, an indispensable part of Near Eastern imagery from ancient times, adds to this level of complexity, and the pace picks up as these combined elements go into action. In Love's drinking bout with the Chinese princess, her darting glance has a hand holding a glass, which is likened to the hand of the angel of death holding the soul: "The hand of her glance held glittering glass / As firm as the soul in Azrail's grasp" (1786). Their intercourse that night is alluded to by the coming together of a round thing with a long thing, of a container with what is contained: "Moon merged in the moonbeam, moonbeam in moon / Wine in the carafe, carafe in wine swooned" (1779). When Beauty first falls for Love, and because he ignores her, suspects that he cares for another, she is likened to a sword of attention waved around in the hand of his roving eye: "A watchful sword in the hand of his glance / Her jealousy led to doubt's hinterland" (422). The representation of a female by the conventionally male image of a sword is an example of another characteristic of the Indian style: reversal. One gets the hang of it.

Notes

[1] My spelling of Ottoman words throughout this book is that of modern Turkish, except for most proper names and terms that have acquired a familiar English spelling—most but not all. For example, I do not use *sheikh* but *Şeyh* as Galip's title: in English usage *sheikh* has acquired so many other, inappropriate meanings, I chose to keep the Turkish spelling. In Ottoman times, a şeyh was an administrative head in a dervish order; in Galip's case, responsible for running a large and influential dervish house, on salary paid by the central administration of the order in Konya. The term includes the meaning of "spiritual adviser" but is not limited to that, and there are other terms for spiritual adviser.

[2] For this reason the sometime translation of the term by which the tribe is named, *muhabbet*, as "friendship" is inappropriate. I have translated both *aşk* and *muhabbet* as "love" in accord with the well-established principle that they are degrees of the same thing (*aşk fart-ı muhabbettir*). The difference in degree relevant to the context of the tale is displayed in the actions of the characters.

[3] I translate *gayret* as "rivalry" in accordance with the principle that God tolerates no *gayr* ("rival"), which is illustrated by the point at which Rivalry disappears in the tale.

[4] The term by which Poetry is named, *suhan* (also written in Turkish as *sühen*), was most often used in Ottoman Turkish to mean "poetry"; it also has the same broader meanings it has in Persian:

"speech," "word," "saying." Gibb (see Bibliographic Note) called the character the Logos, a choice I find at once too generic for Galip's usage and too narrowly Neoplatonistic, in keeping with the characteristically nineteenth-century British orientalist tendency to focus on that single thread of Islamic thought.

[5] The usage "the ninety-nine names of God" refers to a particular ninety-nine of them.

[6] In Turkish, "Peygamber her zaman miracda."

[7] In 1453. Istanbul is the old Greek name of the city, as opposed to various imperial titles by which the city was also known. The Turks did not change the name of the city from Constantinople to Istanbul at that time, as is commonly supposed. To conquer the city was to become the inheritors of "Rum," which to them meant Rome, the West in general.

BIBLIOGRAPHIC NOTE

The considerable interest in Turkish poetry in Europe and Britain during the nineteenth century ended abruptly around the time of the fall of the Ottoman Empire. A new wave of interest began slowly in the 1960s–70s and accelerated in the 1980s and 1990s, but interest is still rare. A bibliography and more detailed information on the topics mentioned in my introduction can be found in my 1994 poetics of the Ottoman romance genre, which may serve as a companion to this edition: *The Unreadable Shores of Love: Turkish Modernity and Mystic Romance* (Austin: U of Texas P, 1994). For more background, and on the lyric in particular, I highly recommend the works of Walter G. Andrews, for example his *Poetry's Voice, Society's Song: Ottoman Lyric Poetry* (Seattle: U of Washington P, 1985) and his collaboration with Najaat Black and Mehmet Kalpaklı, *Ottoman Lyric Poetry: An Anthology* (Austin: U of Texas P, 1997). The nineteenth-century grand narrative of the subject was E. J. W. Gibb's *A History of Ottoman Poetry* (6 vols., ed. Edward G. Browne, London: Luzac, 1900–07). The first new-wave book-length study is Alessio Bombaci's, *La letteratura turca* (Milan, 1965). The volumes of *The Journal of the Muhyiddin Ibn 'Arabi Society* are an excellent guide to the wider philosophical world of *Beauty and Love*.

NOTE ON THE TRANSLATION

A key follows the translation. Proper names and phrases italicized in the translation are explicated there.

I have tried to approximate the Aruz meter of the Turkish text: — —u / u—u— / u——in rhymed couplets. When my rhymes are imperfect, I rhyme with respect only to consonants or only to vowels.

Aruz, like other ancient versification systems such as those of Greek and Latin, is not accentual (based on stress), as in English verse, but quantitative, based on a specific calculation of long (—) and short (u) units, which do not necessarily correspond to syllables, strictly considered. English verse has always been accentual, and after the Norman invasion it incorporated the French and Italian system of strict syllable count, but there have been attempts to write in quantitative meter in English, most notably by Thomas Campion, Shakespeare's contemporary.

The Aruz units are native to Arabic, which has long and short vowels. The units do not exactly correspond to vowel lengths, however. For example, a long unit can be made up of a consonant and a short vowel and a consonant. With license, two short units can take the place of a long unit, especially at the beginning of a line. Aruz was taken from Arabic into Persian and from Persian into Turkish. Turkish does not distinguish between long and short vowels, and so units often more closely correspond to syllables. A similar flexibility applies to the pronunciation of rhyme vowels (vowels are sometimes changed to suit the rhyme). The great majority of poets writing in Arabic, Persian, and Turkish rejected the Aruz system around the time free verse became popular in Europe.

Aruz is a matter of suspension, giving the feeling more of gliding than walking, more of traveling on sea than on land. My approximation often lapses into the merely syllabic, but I have made the attempt to convey the Aruz meter because I am convinced that translation of a strange literature (one new to translation) should preserve a degree of strangeness. To me, translation of Aruz verse into English meters can encourage one to forget that one is reading something really not at all like English verse. Legend has it that Aruz meters were originally based on camel gaits, and one can see why. Iambic pentameter could never be likened to a camel gait.

Galip is known for taking more excessive metrical license than other great Ottoman poets did. Many were famed for the musicality of their verse, but Galip, considered unique for his extraordinary imagery, at times seems to have disdained it.

One other feature of Galip's style I will mention is his mixing of high and low language, refined and colloquial speech, which can create a jarring, even shocking effect of juxtaposition. He also inserted local elements (references to places in Istanbul) into what was traditionally a legendary landscape. These usages are in line with the Indian style, but Galip even went so far as to combine legalese with flip understatement. He often used a knowingly familiar tone, and not only in the nonchalant male speech of a character such as Gayret. Although he made his fluent mastery of intellectual concepts clear, with Galip it is as if he felt that high diction were not good enough for the profound. This attitude is a somewhat different thing from the conviction expressed by the axiom that the truth cannot be expressed in words at all. The height of the Miraj chapter is, "I don't know" (131), and the Turkish expression used, *bilmem*, is the most colloquial way of saying that, almost like, "How should I know?"

ŞEYH GALIP

Beauty and Love

In the name of God, the merciful, the compassionate

For he who had mercy let there be praise   1
He gave dispensation for awe in praise

If not for awe, arduous would be the way
The pen's crooked foot would be stuck in clay

If there's no end to his praises or count
Be thankful the tongue of awe can speak out

Praise be that he gave the spiritual law
The judgment of *dispensation for awe*

He granted the awed comprehension due   5
The dispensation, *"We have not known you ..."*

Else in the end we would still have been awed
But none could have ever reached unto God

He cast his protection o'er our defects
Imposing no burden, nay, but kindness

Not bound *to guide aright*—perish the thought
His bountiful favor never had cause

He created form out of his pure grace
He ordered the world by justice in place

If not for awe we'd be left destitute   10
We would all be stutterers, deaf, dumb, and mute

The posture of praise would be cumbersome
What can a speck of dust say to the sun?

But still we do have the language of awe
We can declare, when we praise him, our awe

Once seen with the fair attention it's due
Is not dispensation for awe a boon?

If every divine gift were glorified
We would ever be in praise occupied

Here too, clearly, is our awe manifest   15
And here, too, the glorious lord forgave us

If we give imagination free range
Then poetry's links will form in a chain

The ocean of thought broke wave upon wave
And frothed up and up amazed and amazed

My heart now is drunk and dazzled henceforth
Since intellect hushed the sea of discourse

In Praise of the *Seyyid* of Creation

The spirits of mankind, though gifts of God
Are dust in the path of the prophets' shah

That shah who reigns on the throne of *not-place*   20
Whose archangels sweep the ground of *not-space*

4

To kiss that shah's foot the moon like a star
Was *split in two* by the force of desire

His gifts are announced by herald Gabriel
And portioned out by his steward, Michael

By *"If not for you"* his essence is praised
The Koran contains and is by it contained

The door to his tent, *the space of two bows*
The rug at his feet, knowledge of both worlds

Shah of Melekut, whose rank is the throne   25
Moon of Jeberut, its shadow below

The waves of the sea of *ahadiyet*
Are one, say the wise, with *Ahmediyet*

His light was *the first created* by God
And so I can say the second of God

Great Adam, the forebear of humanity
In the grove of his prophecy is a tree

When Noah the mourner began to weep
He set sail upon the Prophet's sweet sea

The Nile of constriction rose up apace   30
When Hizir conveyed to Moses his grace

When Abraham seized the sword of his law
He took up the task of smashing false gods

5

Idris taught the host of heaven's residents
About the Miraj of his flawless essence

His beauty is of such priceless degree
They bought Joseph for him in slavery

To give the good news of his coming forth
Ascending the heavenly spheres, Jesus spoke

For him all creation was brought to be   35
The mystery of knowledge, his legacy

The glass of the very oneness of God
The mirror of *things as they really are*

Awaken and come to know the faith true
One prophet, one God, is enough for you

He satiates those who thirst for his grace
His miracles are *with a finger traced*

The musky dark of *he journeyed by night*
Is sovereign seal of his prophethood's right

Though speech be the fountain of miracle   40
The Koran can surely have no parallel

The Koran described the Lord's messenger
Made known to the world his great character

Come now and cut short your tongue, O my pen
God has written all on Tablet with Pen

The Story of the Miraj

A night such that Ummehani's fair home
Would be a vast firmament for that moon

But oh what a night, the guardian of mercy
The sheikh of the Lord's sacred sacristy

Like black-skinned Bilal, possessed of insight   45
The pure light of faith inside of *black light*

As if that night of illustrious effects
Were Veys el-Qarani, light manifest

It came to adore the dust at his foot
As he was called up to the highest good

The shield of the firmament sacrificed
So many a thousand dawns for that night

The night was like immortality's spring
Its black color swelled to break waves of green

The Spring of Nasut brought forth pregnant clouds   50
Green fields of Lahut with joy did resound

In clear view appeared Hizir's fountainhead
The spirits immortal were satiated

The folds of unseen fell in blackout
Sun whispered to moon mysteries without doubt

So sun might display its face to the moon
In cover of darkness light was subsumed

The Nile of astonishment rushed ahead
To bring union's Egypt back from the dead

The heart's speck of *black light* opened out wide   55
Concealing *the journey by night* inside

All things in creation filled up with light
And bright dawn gave birth to morning that night

The sun out of joy was burst in pieces
Stars burning with pleasure lit like torches

Nine heavens were stacked in one heap of light
The brilliance of earth blocked out the sun's sight

Upon the ground of this earth fell such grace
It was all a palace of mirror face

Had sun and moon not been first to step up   60
Stars would have rained down instead of dewdrops

All things in creation were cloaked in light
There for the first time they saw life shine bright

The lost *lamp of night* struck lightning in bolts
Till sunlight and moonlight were dashed to naught

The glittering stars were heaped in a stack
While sun and moon there like fireflies winked back

Black night was a sheltering mirror of light
As lover rejoiced in beloved's sight

God purposed and with volition divine   65
Sent Gabriel with the message divine

As he came descending from heaven's dome
It seemed he rose from the dust to God's throne

That greatest archangel brought him a mount
"O most noble messenger," he announced

"This is your steed, named Burak the unique
The throne most sublime has come to your feet

Come visit the throne, view heaven's broad space
Do not disappoint the realm of *not-place*"

The goal of creation by command, *"Be!"*   70
Bowed then to obey the divine decree

Each thing hastens back to race to its source
And so the *Koran* saw heaven once more

His royal foot then upon stirrup pressed
His saddle was the abode of oneness

No thing, neither space nor time, could endure
As naught became this bird's nest called the world

The sea of unicity stirred and rose
As meaning was interchanged there with form

The mystery of unity entered in form   75
Original meaning found there a form

And there on Jerusalem's sacred ground
The mystery of servanthood to be found

He bowed down and God the truth was bowed to
The station of the unseen witnessed to

The spirits of the prophets came to pray
And then what occurred God only can say

O pen, come now, do not race on so fast
The mysteries of prophecy cannot be grasped

Since when can a dewdrop speak for the sea?   80
Since when can men worthy of God's work be?

Get back to the poet's usual style
Leave off all this Sufi talk for a while

The Prophet stepped on the *first firmament*
The pretty moon split into two fragments

So people should clearly see the abstract
The *age of the moon,* the age of Ahmet

Since on the Miraj time does not exist
One cannot speak of a time before it

The moon's *splitting* by his miracle *in two*   85
In truth was *the rending of his breast*'s proof

When Gabriel took that sore heart in hand
He healed him completely and made him prance

The archangels served as royal escorts
And cried, "God is with you!," with dancing hearts

With heavenly inspiration's accord
He came to the sphere of Mercury's court

Hassan bin Sabit, the poet sublime
Beseeched that shah for his pardon this time

Absolving Hassan there for his black verse   90
He pardoned him for the sin of his words

Then God who guides cleared his deputy's way
To the third sphere of Venus, known as Zuhre

She called on his daughter Zehra so fair
And so obtained of his pardon a share

He journeyed on to the fourth firmament
Where pride doubled up the four elements

The Messiah, by grace of sweet Muhammad
Became as if once more resurrected

Night's lamp ever-living hurled lightning forth   95
The sun wished the earth would swallow it up

He took the fifth heaven then for mansion
And Mars felt his heart in sore contraction

Mars wept blood and sang a tune of regret
He stained the broad skirt of heaven rose red

That Shah who rides on the spheres forgave him
He pardoned the angel of death his sin

The six directions then made their request
And on to the sixth sphere he then progressed

Then so that thereby the seven climes' shah   100
Should give *heaven's judge* lessons in the law

In the name of God the Truth he revealed
That judgments of bygone days were repealed

Augury and astrology were disgraced
Sites and what they *manifest* put in place

And thus from the seventh heavenly perch
He granted joy to the whole universe

Black Saturn asked Bilal to intercede
Prostrating himself, he thus made his plea:

"Enough for tonight this request of mine: 105
Let black of all colors be most sublime"

So that padishah of *"If not for you"*
His tour of the heavenly spheres did conclude

But still the Miraj of God's gracious gift
Was not yet complete *as it really is*

When toward heaven's throne he set his foot down
With joy the sphere of the fixed stars whirled round

It was for the sake of this visit that
God mounted the sphere of the zodiac

His person immaculate, soaring up high   110
Drew Taurus the earthbound up to the sky

That Shah without peer great favor bestowed
And let Gemini be lord of his robe

When Libra then stretched his palm out to beg
He filled it not with coin, but pearls instead

And Pisces bowed groveling down at his feet
While Cancer dove into mystery's deep

When Leo recalled his cousin to mind
He gained his release through Ali the Lion

Because Aries, offering up his complaint   115
Did many tales of his courage relate

Aquarius cried, his heart in his hand:
"Oh but one drop for the sake of Zamzam!"

The grace he received then went to his head
He cried like the waterwheel, "Muhammad!"

The Pleiades, strung round Capricorn's neck,
He sent to his two grandsons as a gift

That night full of mystery Gabriel's wing
Took flight up from Virgo again and again

Since heaven's clock has need of Scorpio   120
In time he made his petition also

He found the grace of acceptance and peace
And not for an instant did honor cease

Zal looked at his Sagittarian bow
Now weak, by the passage of time brought low

Astride *the space of two bows* now that shah
Pressed on beyond the two worlds further on

He kept trusted Gabriel close by his side
As far as the heavenly throne to abide

He saw Tablet, Cherubim, and Pen too   125
Mysteries by the thousand were in plain view

God's throne in its joy was so struck with awe
It lost track completely of where it was

The throne like a shadow now left behind
Throne-ranked, "To the Lord of the throne!" he cried

And what lies beyond then came to be seen
They journeyed as far as the Sidre tree

The gate there to union's sanctum swung free
Nearness left behind, now came unity

Then Gabriel was by awe overcome   130
All words by their meanings were abandoned

What he became, what he was, I don't know
He overflowed—what was filled, I don't know

O merciful God whose mercy flows free
Please gladden your servant with your reprieve

He wishes from you eternal success
That is to say, pauper Galip Esat

Is one of your people, although in sin
His hope is you'll grant him intercession

If not for your gift of intercession   135
Many pious men would meet a bad end

Since I am a man of pride, black in deeds
I will have good news for each aim I seek

In Praise of Hazret-i Hudavengâr

Since God set the seal upon the prophets
Enlightened friends of God have come to us

Shah to that group is the Sovereign Molla
This world has one single world-conqueror

Sultan of the throne of insight's kingdom
Seated on the prayer mat of God's Lion

His thought shows the road to reality   140
His likeness would be Siddiq's deputy

Sun of the sky of the sons of Hayder
He treads the *golden chain* of Gazanfer

He made the pen cut of reed bear witness
So we'd know what the song of David was

He surpassed the learned in excellence
Worthy to be called prophet of the west

His discourse has Jesus's spirit for soul
And like the Messiah revives the law

No book but his *Masnavi* has been named   145
Gist of the Koran—behold now its fame

The city most great is his poetry's land
Enthroned in a corner, Ibn Adham

A man of Ibrahim Gulshani's scale
Wails in that grove like a lone nightingale

The *abdal* of heaven swoon for his love
Sun and moon are Sineçak for his love

His eloquent couplets, verse upon verse
Are mysteries of the law and the truth

His poetry lights the lamp of meaning   150
Each point is a *lamp of night* of meaning

16

A crown for the flock of the friends of God
Shah and nobleman of the pure of heart

His ocean encircles both East and West
In waves of immersion and discernment

His dominion ranges through every clime
His grace running through divisions of time

The world is filled with the grace of his aid
Don't talk of his miracles—all is vain

In Praise of My Father

In setting a seal upon this discourse   155
A praiseworthy gentleman was the cause

A man bowed upon the path of glory
Namely my father, Reshid Efendi

Secluded within the heart's prayer room
He gambles his head for the saint of Rum

The truth is I had been mute and speechless
I had lost the power of eloquence

The tongue of my pen had fallen silent
A thousand waves broke of deep discontent

I had become weary of words and talk   160
Scent and color were abandoned by thought

The chapter of the Miraj not yet down
This *Beauty and Love* was left without crown

He told me to persevere, he said, "Speak"
By grace of his breath this work is complete

He took my hand when I'd wandered astray
He taught to me poetry in Rumi's way

That warrior took me under his wing
And filled me up with life's eternal spring

Since he was my guide to love's universe   165
As father is not twofold his service?

Whatever I may say in praise of him
Is free from stain of hypocrisy's sin

That noble man held me when I was mute
And with his breath made me sing like the flute

He was both the cause, and by his effort
Many were the spiritual masters I served

Denial of the wonders of his effect
Is blasphemy—I was resurrected

He knows, but he would not call this favor   170
And I will not be complacent either

The sea of God's favor has no beyond
There's many a pearl of grace to be found

If't please the compassionate, merciful being
The mysteries of witness will yet be seen

The Reason for This Composition

As one of an intimate circle of friends
I was Adam in the garden again

Our gatherings were rose gardens of love
Whose nightingales sang of friendship and love

All poets, jewelers of words to a man   175
All young, bearing with them treasures in hand

They talked poetry, virtue, consciousness
Their bonds were verse, prose, and keen awareness

I'd lost my head with the first draught of truth
The time was the early dawn of fresh youth

There Nabi's *Beneficity* was read
The poet was said to stand in good stead

In truth, it is a most curious work
Much valued by those who study the book

He wrote it while he was in his old age   180
When he was mature and become a sage

When one of our number known for fine verse
Extravagantly made much praise of the work

Each and every poet present declared
This judgment was most approvingly shared

They carried their praises to such extreme
No poet could match the verse of Nabi

That cup felt a trifle much to my hand
It seemed to me that a challenge was planned

With veiled irony I made to object   185
And answered the group's praise in this respect:

"Should Nabi then ever have cause to gloat
For piling words on those Sheikh Attar spoke?

You don't know his work, *Divinity's Book*?
Was there something he left out of that book?

That's all there to the story, my friend
The rest of it is all lies without end

A Persianate work of couplets in rhyme
A long chain of genitives linked in rhyme

Though Arabic prose may thus be adorned   190
In Turkish it is but tediously borne

There'd have been no harm if he'd kept it short
Perhaps we'd have called that art of a sort

There's this moreover, that craftsman of words
In hyperbole's a low-flying bird

He lauds Burak, pride of the universe
But Nefi's *Rahshiye* is better verse

Was there need to load Burak with such praise?
Who told him he should thus lengthen his days?

Forgive him, one may not know, or forget   195
You don't kill a fine horse for one false step

But there is this too: that venerable sage
Enjoyed the fame and acclaim of his age

Five great shahs like angels in ancestry
Supported his talent generously

He'd gained his desire in this world's bazaar
He'd won fame on poetry's field of fire

And then to indulge in gross indolence
Shows in many ways such unworthiness

He finds a few pleasant figures of speech   200
For a wedding—is this a worthy man's reach?

But you'll say that venerable Nizami
He too undertook this, favorably

No cause for surprise, that's the Persian style
Persian savants don't observe proper style

There's no need to be content with their lead
Acceptable, but why try to exceed

There's this too, although he weighs his words well
His pen found no treasure, just much travail

His hero's a barefoot thief—as if he   205
Would climb with Mansur up the gallows tree

Concocting a fabulous Miraj night
He'd have him ascend to heaven with Christ

The structure of Nabi's story is based
Upon the ascension of a false knave

The story was fingered, if truth be told
And thieves are rewarded for being bold

He strained in his dotage, that's all he left
And worse, glorified the knave's work of theft

If he gives advice, it's this he finds wise: 210
'This world will pass, the afterlife abides'

No matter how deaf or lacking in wit
There can be no ear that has not heard this

They call him a man who breaks a new trail
Enlightening those already aware

His statement should not be mere platitude
With infinite care his work will bear fruit

But who is there I could share this much with?
If only I could know even just this!

If what I say fell upon others' lips   215
Would I need to search the heavens like this?

Oh dear, what complaint is this I've disclosed
I should repent a hundred thousandfold!

The one bright verse praised by one poet true
To that verse a thousand heavens are due

The pen in my hand does ever repeat
'The praise of the mass is ruin to me'

Its work is to offer strength and support
To cherish with understanding rapport

Of course the faculties will dull with time   220
The tongue grow too weak to speak the sublime

But still talent shines forth obviously
One's inheritance there for all to see

A man who's aware and quick to perceive
Would never have shah be equal with thief

However assailed by age and abuse
A falcon does not resemble a goose

Shall it come to pass that love's rapture fail?
Has there finally been an end to that tale?

Is there anything but love that deserves   225
The spending for its sake pearls of words?

You'll say it's been retold time after time
Do not weary of life's eternal wine

The world's all a tale of love and friendship
The rest is despair, bad luck and hardship

If you have become aware of this path
No bandit can waylay you on this path

This is poetry's ineffable pain
I cannot describe all that it contains

A guard who stands watch at art's treasure case   230
Has no art that talent finds to its taste"

One blessed with Messiah's breath at last said
"I neither approve nor write one instead"

I tried to object and not to relent
I offered support for each argument

This tune I began to sing there that day
At first put me in a difficult way

My friends held me to my word, saying, "Come,
You've staked your claim, now there's work to be done

That which Nabi with great effort obtained   235
God granted you in your youth to attain"

With that desire then to make good my word
I took pen in hand and wrote this patched verse

There are flaws I do concede, but maintain
Still I do not speak entirely in vain

Though the color's off, it's Indian quilt
And won't be worth less than Aleppo silk

Who comes from the city of friendship wise
Will know the true source of our merchandise

The Story Begins

Awakened by grace of Shams of Tabriz   240
The pen cut of Rumi's sugar-sweet reed

Relates thus its declaration of love
And tells me the epic tale of its love

There once was among the Arabs a tribe
In whom the fine virtues all coincide

First leaf of the book of *youth sworn to serve*
First tribe among Arabs, the Sons of Love

But oh what a tribe!—pain's own prayer niche
Their faces were pale, their luck black as pitch

The sun of July served them for attire   245
Their drink of flame set the whole world on fire

Their valleys were strewn with grief's shattered glass
And sorrows as many as grains of sand

Their sighs of privation served them for tents
Like flutes they conversed in wails and laments

Each and every one was stricken by love
Their mouths were as red as swords dripping blood

Their sustenance was the unforeseen test
Fire rained down upon their heads without rest

They planted for seed red-hot searing sparks   250
And reaped at the harvest time shredded hearts

All those who with spirit bring speech to life
Concur that Majnun was kin to that tribe

Each person who courts the ordeal most harsh
Is joined—of this be sure—to that same hearth

They sold the commodity of life for hire
And purchased the smoldering burn of desire

The Sons of Love at Their Feasts

When they came to feast and take ease from toil
A storm of trial set the cook pot to boil

For cups they raised clubs with mountainous heads   255
And drank down the wine of bloodcurdling death

Their parties were killing fields where men vied
Their music, breast-beating clamor and cries

They thought a stiletto a long-stemmed glass
And mistook for silk their wretched torn rags

The angel of death was their own *saki*
And Mars was the boy who danced at their feast

Wild shouts of lament were zither and drum
Dread soul-chilling fever, tambourine man

The sweetmeats and nuts they nibbled with drinks   260
Were poisonous loss and evil-eye jinx

Their bottles were corked with stuff drenched in blood
Their wounds flowed with streams of fire in a flood

Such torture and suffering, moans and laments
Could pleasure require more fit instruments?

The Sons of Love at the Hunt

When these men set out to hunt prey and track
They went nowhere from which one could come back

They caught scrawny lizards for birds of prey
And winged scorpions instead of plump quail

Their pained looks of longing, falcons in flight   265
Caught omens and owls that hooted at night

A dragon coiled up and ready to strike
They thought a migration of cranes in flight

Their deer were the smoke of riotous sighs
With bodies burnt black and antlers of fire

These hunters were struck with love for their prey
They thought hares were bullets speeding away

A man tried to shoot an arrow afar
But drew himself on his bow like a dart

They shot vipers using snakes as their shafts   270
Drawn from their own faces for quiver bags

The Sons of Love in Springtime

When springtime came blooming into that place
Headlong to the desert everyone raced

Their wounds effused sighs so high that when linked
They shot to the mountains fast as lightning

They had in mind only liquid that flowed
A stream or a gash in flesh—who would know

Some thought night fell when they saw the night flowers
Some thought scorpions were hyacinth flowers

They thought a heart's wound a bed of rose   275
    blooms
They thought bloody streams were fallen red blooms

Each man wandered round the edge of the woods
And plucked not spring tulips, but his own wounds

No man could enjoy a bright flower bed
His heart was robbed by some charmer again

A pomegranate? What's that? No one knew
Was fire the thing that the flower beds grew?

Do roses laugh? Do the flowering trees cry?
Are these fresh young saplings weeping blood? Why?

Is this wailing from nightingale or rose?   280
Do hyacinths make one's mind scattered so?

The stream, why's he bound and shackled in chains?
He won't be still, who made him writhe in pain?

The willow, why do his arms droop and cling?
The pheasant won't take him under her wing?

What ails the narcissus, he looks so grim
Won't his lover deign to look upon him?

Is it fire of passion raining down doom?
Is it longing that makes rose flowers bloom?

They knew of no difference 'tween earth and   285
    skies
A rose garden looked like stars to their eyes

29

They wandered from place to place like Majnun
They scattered, disheveled, all in a swoon

Imagine their seasons by spring compared
Don't make me describe their autumns—beware!

An Event Most Strange

One night then among the men of this tribe
A state most exceeding strange did arise

A thousand fates were brought forth on that night
The stars and the skies were filled up with fright

The heavens collided one with the next   290
Some angels were laughing while others wept

Rejoicings a thousandfold, fear and awe
Church bells, temple drums, and cries of "Allah!"

A drumming resounded on heaven's roof
A quaking upon the face of the earth

First, thick folds of darkness, layer upon layer
Then light raining down, dispersed everywhere

Each tree, every blade of grass bowed in awe
Amazed, rivers melted, fled and ran off

Now there were a thousand threatening shapes   295
Now horror and hope broke crashing in waves

Conjunctions were formed between star and star
A rain of elation, then hail of horror

Inside of the dark a riotous din
The desperate screaming of kith and kin

This torturous contagion spread among all
While joy became relative, not real at all

The heavens resounding echoed boom! boom!
The earth disappeared, swallowed up in gloom

The Birth of Beauty and Love

That night in this palace bright of the earth   300
There set foot two babes of high, noble birth

And suddenly then the dawn of hope glowed
The sun and the moon together both rose

Born mounted on sun and moon these two shahs
Were both, it seems, of those strange events cause

But one was a girl with jasmine-bright breast
The other a boy whose face shone like Christ's

The tribe comprehended what had transpired
All heard about these two destined for trial

They chose for the girl the name of Beauty   305
The chosen son was named Love unhappy

31

As time went on, some called Beauty Leyla
Some called her Shirin, and others Azra

Then some gave the name of Majnun to Love
Some called him Vamik, and others Ferhad

And then that song took on a different tune
They called Love Leyla and Beauty Majnun

Fate broke its enchantment thus day by day
And shuffled their names in some other way

While these two were still but innocent babes   310
The skies whirled to make them misplace their names

That famous for namelessness they would win
Disorientation as discipline

The Betrothal of Beauty and Love

A gracious feast was prepared with great care
The lords of the tribe were all gathered there

The lords cast their votes for these two moons so:
They'd be one another's, willing or no

Their fathers would be convinced to agree
That from this time forth thus all prayers would be

This outcome had been decided by fate   315
The meeting was closed without more debate

How Love Passed the Time; or, Love's Upbringing

The infant Love started to writhe and twist
Bound up in the swaddling ties of anguish

The whirling sky rich in dread misfortune
Had fashioned his cradle from a coffin

The easier sleep might come to his eye
His nurse composed for him this lullaby:

Lyric

Sleep, sleep, O moon that tonight you may hear
The cry of "O Lord" nestled in your ear
Although their intention is not yet clear   320
The stars' verdict surely does thus appear
You'll roast on a turning skewer of blame

Sleep, sleep, my rosebud, there's but little time
What fate has in store for you is malign
It's ruthless and violent, quick and ill-timed
It's but illusion to think fate benign
My fear is that you will wither away

Narcissus of Love, keep distant in sleep
Fall down upon destiny's skirt and entreat
The soul's eye wide, a thousand fears heed   325
Beware consequences trial will unleash
You will be the plaything of circling change

Come now and rest in the cradle of ease
Enjoy a few precious short nights of peace
Consider your end and be gracious please
Leave milk and make blood the drink of your ease
You'll drink the dregs of the cup of ill fame

Sleep inside your cradle, my jasmine-breast
The wheel of fate won't at this one point rest
The stars don't continue the same progress   330
Watch what will befall you at their behest
You'll turn like a mill at the stream of pain

Don't make it your custom to lie awake
Sleep, if anything, will come to your aid
The heaven's deathsman will serve up nightshade
Like Galip, cries and wails will be your trade
You'll be fiddle for the feast of complaint

Lying in his cradle that jasmine-breast ruin
Was as shining sun on a crescent moon

Each minute the cradle rocked to and fro   335
He gleamed like quicksilver he trembled so

That bright star of hope was all in a shiver
The sun's image dancing inside a mirror

Alike the moon of Nahsheb in the well
Or as the sun would in Scorpio dwell

Sometimes in his cradle he became peeved
A gleaming sword rattling inside its sheath

While inside his cradle that tempest slept
In body the spirit found and gained strength

Gazelle-like he was the light of the eye   340
Within the arch of the brow strung to fly

Or one would have said that babe were Jesus
The cradle sublime for him a prayer niche

But still he was wearied with discontent
As if on the bed of ease he were spent

He didn't for long in one pose remain
He trembled, his body like to a flame

Sometimes when he seemed to be in ill mood
They'd say it was drunken sleep made him brood

That rose-figured fire, to sum up in fine   345
In this agitation passed all his time

How Beauty Passed the Time

For Beauty, too, infelicitous fate
Decreed that her cradle shiver and shake

The tyrant of fortune to her also
Habitual change perverse did bestow

While brooding she'd brighten with a gay air
Amidst pleasure plunge deep into despair

To all she appeared decorously grave
While sleep to her eyes she strictly forbade

Like treason she seethed, that pretty despot   350
Fate thought it amusing to wake her up

Let us dispense with the need for detail
Which could much fatigue and boredom entail

It's not suitable that lovers should be
Dumbstruck and bedazzled when they first meet

The First Signs Appear

In this manner months and years passed away
Till suffering would no more be delayed

The lords of the tribe were gathered once more
To vote and light candles in firm accord

That blessed with keen wit these two lively tots   355
Should wax full as moons acquiring the arts

The fund of desire is by art endowed
The head's humble bow will be the head's crown

Once learning to know the moon full and bright
One finds little star Suha in the night

Beauty and Love Go to School

Two almond hearts entered into one husk
And came to the school called Proper Conduct

Two baby half couplets joined in one verse
And opened a poem of subtle converse

Two bewitching eyes read spellbinding vows   360
School desks arched before their glances like brows

Split-tongued *like a pen*, one heart in discourse
Together they made one single discourse

Two camphor-white candles shined as one light
That school was a crystal mansion of light

The school was the common substance they shared
Two meanings came in to take one form there

One branch sprouted two new rosebuds in flower
Each one playing nightingale to the other

They two grafted there were joined up as one   365
In that blossom lapping up the same blood

They'd cite quotes to illustrate points they made
And thus mirror sun and moon in a frame

When they sat together two in one place
The mirror both man and image contained

The school was that sacred house of the one
Where loss and attainment do meet as one

Shy eyes gazed full of hopes unrealized
Like male and female slaves in paradise

Let sun and moon frolic in heaven's place   370
The moth and the flame, the lampshade of space

Between them the union of warp and woof
Was woven of awed and innocent looks

Their lessons, resigned and submissive ways
Their tutor, Professor Madness the sage

Professor Madness

What madness—behold the perfected sheikh
A jurisconsult of rationalist states

Alone in the valley of the absurd
Transcending the bounds of possible worlds

He brought to the night of ignorance dawn   375
With him prohibitions all were reformed

He'd never climb out on thought's fragile limb
Or fall on thought's stones—what was that to him?

His actions were far from wherefore and why
In faithlessness or faith he was not tried

To him shah and beggar were both the same
The discourse of reason, idle ill fame

Alone an all-powerful shah he did stand
All matters proceeded by his command

He harbored nor doubt nor uncertainty 380
The universe held no more mystery

He'd mount a revolt even against God
No fire could burn him, he feared no harm

A sovereign sultan uniquely alone
He had soldiers *naked* all of his own

His premise arose from his conclusion
His analogy could make parts of the one

When he discoursed he silenced all the world
He made the wise understand with one word

He thrust Ibn Melek underground in shame 385
And found Fahreddin a thousand ways lame

When he saw the turban of Imad famed
He coined Hajji Turnip for his nickname

Mirza Jan would strum the lute at his feasts
Fahr-i Jurjan led drunkards' dancing feet

Sheikh of Islam in the harsh clime of trial
His word no decree could subject to trial

Dread Satan, a blind man begging his boon
At court, Aristotle played his buffoon

Beauty Falls in Love with Love

By cruel decree of unfavorable fate   390
Beauty fell in love with Love's shining face

Fair Beauty adorns the world thousandfold
But like Zuleyha gave Joseph her soul

A lover when she beloved should be
A Vamik when she an Azra should be

Love's countenance and the love of his face
Brought autumn's dog rose to bloom in her face

The letter *alif* brought his height to mind
As high as the heavenly throne rose her sigh

Jeem was a sign for the curl on his brow   395
Its point proved a thousand things to her now

Frightful to her did *ra* dagger-like seem
Her lips trembled so she could not say *meem*

With sharp teeth the saw-like-faced letter *seen*
Mowed down her youth like a tender sapling

Her *thirtieth of the Koran* a moon face
Like freckles the writing strewn everyplace

Most students make schoolwork their one concern
But love was the lesson these children learned

About Their Love

Come let your fancy that garden compose 400
Where candle is nightingale and moth is rose

The blood of sweet ruby lips warmed for Love
Shirin would now give her life for Ferhad

Like parrots her sugary lips chattered of
The soul of a lover in the beloved

His Leyla mad with her dreams of Majnun
The candle wept blood for moth in a swoon

She shook down her tresses over her cheeks
His rose kiss made wounds split open her cheeks

Her ruby lips parted for a remark 405
Desire tore the rose's petals apart

She could not speak, though modesty forbade
The gem of her secret was plain as day

Beauty's every word was friendship and love
And Love only could be dazzled in awe

His majesty Love appeared to be cool
While drinking in all things like a whirlpool

41

He loves her, he loves her not, no one knew
Though one couldn't say he hadn't a clue

Silent he was, he neither sighed nor moaned   410
Bewildered, he knew neither rule nor road

He was mirror-like, that ravishing rogue
A form unique without speech, without soul

The more that he looked, he drew Beauty in
Attracting the sun of Beauty to him

That moon of Nahsheb was the solar disk
All naught but a gaze, without ear or lip

As Beauty rose bright like fire in a blaze
God only knew who would burn in that blaze

As Beauty grew feeble as tears she wept   415
Each sigh was a maelstrom ring round her neck

Her head bowed like a decanter to Love
She seemed crystal, he an earthenware jug

This much was clear, Beauty's broken heart bled
While he appeared to be a piece of lead

The longing she felt an impossible thing
What did Love have in mind? ... mystifying

Gazelle-like, bad-tempered, swift on the run
He would not stoop to approach anyone

That spellbinder made Beauty lose her wits   420
She was a well-laid snare scattered to bits

Love's eyes narrowed in a languorous look
Amazed and confused, the darling's soul shook

A watchful sword in the hand of his glance
Her jealousy led to doubt's hinterland

She'd say: "Won't contentious fate find it meet
To make him want me, the dust at his feet?

It's clear that it's someone else he longs for
What sort of prey is he then hunting for?

If he loves the moon, let me be the sky   425
Let me be a star if his love is the sky

What goddess does he see in his mind there?
Can't I make a Magian belt of my hair?

If I knew what was the idol he served
I'd be like a Brahmin ready to serve"

Sometimes she'd reflect upon this and thought
"What have I said? I take refuge in God!

Is there no star in all heaven to move
The sun to petition love to the moon?

If I, moon, do not his fond love inspire   430
Would he then pay court to Suha's faint fire?"

Still Beauty who ornaments the whole world
Did not reveal this affair to the world

She locked her doubts tightly inside her breast
She'd never give that moon-cheeked boy offense

Her name, yes, was Beauty, flawless Beauty
But what was that peerless boy, what was he?

On the Qualities of Beauty

A tulip cheek framed by raven ringlets
A rosebud surrounded by hyacinths

Her breast a quicksilver sea of mirror   435
A string of pearls like a whirlpool lay there

Without doubt her pretty mouth and her teeth
Were pearls and gems, treasures of the *unseen*

Her mouth had to miracle exclusive right
One point explicating *the verse of light*

The silvery cup of youth's deathless spring
Was thirsty with awe for her dimpled chin

Her falcon eyes surprised the soul within
Entrancing like deer, or skittish pigeons

Her delicate arm, a silvery branch   440
All kneaded from dough of roses perchance

Her fingers were camphor candles pure white
With henna-rose petals on tips of light

Her proud lofty stature raised up the dead
Severe heaven smiled upon her proud head

Her movements the terror of judgment day
Her curls waved like flags declaring its sway

Red rubies and pearls thirst for her discourse
Though gems, her lips were possessed of discourse

Her brows drew swords on the curls of her hair   445
And thrust aside flanks of chains woven there

Her languid glance swore revenge on the soul
Against faith her raven tresses waged war

Her pure and white breast resplendent with light
Resembled the beams of morning sunlight

Her neck was a cypress gracing a stream
It shone on the Bosphorus like a moonbeam

Her earlobes were rosy like morning light
The sun served her for an earring by night

Those hands clothed in archer's bejeweled gloves   450
With one single shot maimed all the sun's claws

Hope's festival dawned upon her fresh cheek
The eye of the sun bled rouge for her cheek

Her arms, the immortal stream of Kevser
Her fingers were abstract essences there

The Pleiades and the sky's other stars
Were strung round her neck like jewels and pearls

Her long tresses were a raw amber hoard
The mole on her cheek, its black Hindu guard

Her breasts were like oranges from heaven's grove   455
Her eyes gazed with longing on them below

With henna that fairy painted her heel
And made reddest wine trip, stumble and reel

Her lip's ruby was a jewel dripping sweet
And rosy moonbeams the lamp of her cheek

The brows of her forehead dazzled the mind
Her lashes shot spears deluding the mind

Her pink cheeks were rubies wrapped in white fluff
Her mouth made by silence meaning enough

The soul of her lip, the essence of speech   460
A smile's paradise bloomed on her rose cheek

Those sorceress eyes took up sword in hand
And guarded the treasures of Capriceland

The black mole poised at the edge of her mouth
Hunted for gold like a Moroccan scout

Her eyelashes cast her cheeks in shadow
And made her form shiver from head to toe

Sage poet Nizami seemed with this verse
To characterize her lashes and curls:

"Desiring a kiss, her curls swept aside   465
Her eyelashes whispered, 'Let God provide'"

Her lip's ruby was a flame sugar-fed
Her rose cheeks were spring decked in rosy red

That luminous neck, that bosom so pure
A candle of camphor lit in a mirror

Her breast was a treasure box, a charmed cache
Erjeng's paintings framed in a looking glass

Her sweet lips resembled rosebuds of light
Where bees joined with moths to buzz round by night

Her glance was a piercing fiery dart   470
Her lance of reproach like fate struck its mark

Her image would satiate inspired grace
Her speech left profound mystery outraced

The blood of a peacock dyed her robe rouge
Her coquetry had its own thousand hues

The Kingdom of Groans fell at her command
Her style was a rose bed in Sugarland

Her frown of reproach all hope would destroy
The boon of her kindness, eternal joy

If Hizir had found the balm of her eyes   475
Pitch darkness would have seemed eternal life

Her ringlets made oaths of union to hearts
Her sharp glances then swore severance harsh

The curls scattered there upon her forehead
For sufferers sealed the penalty of death

She taxed the shah of the Land of Caprice
And pillaged the clime of those who entreat

Her tresses made raids on musk's caravan
And strung up their plunder on every strand

Her bangs both to heart and faith brought   480
   downfall
She kept China and Not-China in thrall

Her black eyes and delicately curved brows
Inscribed in a prayer niche two divine vows

Her black mole brought ruin to every man
Made rebels of Zanzibar and Sudan

Doe-eyed Leylas by the thousand would swoon
Enthralled by her fantasies of Majnun

Her curls held a thousand souls by a thread
In warp and woof of the will to forget

How many enlightened souls for that face   485
Shout out invocations of divine grace

All delicacy, subtlety, all of a piece
Sweet gentleness, loveliness, without cease

O pen, may God bless you a thousand times
To Beauty's charms you have opened your eyes

You've called to mind and you've sung that moon's
        praise
You've honored the perfect style of her ways

Your purpose with verse is a work of art
So speak now of Love—that too is an art

On the Qualities of Love

A countenance shining like a dark moon   490
Behind veils the spring of eternal youth

The gleam of a tempered sword for a beard
Black moonlight that falls in spring on Kashmir

His garden of grief left Hizir of insight
To drink down the poison of worldly life

Faced with his proud look no power could hold out
Poor Gabriel was a half-slaughtered fowl

His glance of death's angel ravished the soul
Mischief came to slaughter in a blindfold

The fuzz of his cheek, smoke from Nimrod's fire   495
His ruby lips stained Kevser spring with wine

Horizons would be destroyed round the world
Had not his beard tamed his serpent-like curls

The discourse of Jesus in his eye hid
One word from him raised cruel fate from the dead

His drunken glance was a sword keen and fine
He quaffed tears of houris for ruby wine

From under his cap a curly fringe fell
To God's greatest name across the moon spell

A sun, sword in hand, he rained bloody light   500
Submerging the martyrs of God in light

When curls at his temples taught spells of awe
His glance cried out, "We take refuge in God!"

Injustice wreaked by the look in his eye
Would make Jesus take death's daughter for bride

The fuzz round his lips, the light of God's word
A gospel like Christ revealed to the world

Take refuge in God, so careless he'd be
The angel of death begged on bended knee

The hangman there in his gaze now behold   505
An angel of death bestowing the soul

His lips were such when he spoke the word "love"
Accustomed like dawn to drinking down blood

His lashes would flutter just slightly so
And send forth a thousand soldiers of woe

The spirit of his discourse granted life
But for those who loved him, haphazard strife

None could comprehend the light of his face
The sun next to him a handful of clay

His mouth's essence was mysterious Lahut   510
His every vow a mirage of Nasut

He showed a disdain of such cruel degree
His ear would not hear *Show yourself to me*

His lovers despised guests and social calls
His lashes slapped the sun's face with their claws

So callous, for him Jacob's tears of blood
Were rouge for the young bride's cheek that he loved

His lovers wailed at his feasts like the reed
In chorus God's words *You shall not see me*

He strapped to his saddle faith's bird as prey   515
The threads of its life left in disarray

The curve of his mouth was intellect's death writ
His glance made the soul of piety forfeit

His mastered disdain's sword lip with a word
His vow's fulfillment unjust as his word

His sword a peacock in blood's paradise
His ax a bell tolling for faith's demise

For heaven's Shebdiz the sun of Khusrev
The crescent moon in his saddle would nest

His lovers were as infirm as his word   520
Their bodies like bubbles ready to burst

Famed for eloquence, the poet Neshet
Recounted his beauty with this couplet:

"The sky was shade for the lamp of his soul
The moths there were angels none could console"

If heaven were all a piece the sun's orb
The crescent moon would mime his eyebrow's curve

His beard framed the brilliant lines of his face
As if the sun were to dawn in black space

Reclined on the moon if Venus would speak   525
She'd be a match for the mole on his cheek

If *black light* were shred and torn bit by bit
I'd not liken those curls even to it

If Jesus drank Hizir's fountain of youth
The down on Love's lip would have other truth

If Mary had carried Joseph instead
She'd have borne a twin for Love's handsome head

If rosebuds of light were of soul possessed
They'd gather like bees for his lips' caress

If faith took with infidelity one form   530
They would to the writ of his beard conform

If Hulagu gained the Messiah's grace
He would say his prayers to that roving gaze

The beard on his cheek perfumed ambergris
An infidel housed in heaven supreme

On that cheek the stray curl he would ignore
A hyacinth strewn on fire's threshing floor

That sorcerer of his look knew no fear
Who was Gabriel and who Jesus here?

He'd not in a foul mood crave tyranny   535
Else where would this seven-tiered heaven be?

He'd not give his glance permission to raid
Else naught of faith or the world would remain

He'd set out to loose a flood tide of cares
But take pity on the children of tears

Should his Noah's grief say *"None without faith"*
Pharoah would be drowned in a flood of faith

Should his Harut's glance suggest his ill will
Zuleyha would fall into Joseph's well

Should blasphemy be charged to destroy faith   540
It would do so by leave of his black gaze

The heart lit by candle of his desire
Would have the lice of Job flit round its fire

In his love's slave market Joseph was left
Stained with the blood of a hundred regrets

His lovers took Solomon's seal of command
To stamp themselves and adorn their *white hands*

His cheek was a blazing sun of pure fire
The resplendent sun aglow inside fire

Beauty Visits Love's Room from Time to Time

Saki, I am brainless, be generous please   545
My feet are bound up with ribbons of ease

Bring wine, there's no cure for this malady
No shore to the ocean of poetry

Shall this sea remain becalmed, pure surface?
Shall I then not speak? Please, do me justice!

Because you begrudge wine's inspiring light
You keep the moon of my heart blocked from sight

Fear spiky sharp shards of our shattered hearts
Beware, keep your silk away from our sparks

An ocean's desire is flooding my head   550
What's there in a word, it's only one breath

I'm helpless, O Saki, come to my aid
At misfortune's bazaar I chose heartache

There are many coins of speech I require
To buy up the merchandise of desire

Speech, yes, but the discourse of drunkenness
Of failure and loss, defeat and distress

Bring wine, for I now have no more words left
The stock of my longing has all been spent

It's so very hard while here at the start   555
The preface of mystery still left to start

Bring wine, O my rose of delicacy
And ask me what tale I shall tell to thee

The *saki* who serves wine at meaning's feast
Then granted with this joy spirit replete:

While Beauty increased her need day by day
Her heart like the moon bled more day by day

Love multiplied the torments of her heart
A thousand thoughts and dreams worried her heart

Her beauty was amplified as she grieved   560
She took on a different luster and sheen

This sheen caused a trembling throughout her form
She was mirror but quicksilver in form

Bright flame filled the wineglass up to the brim
Her cheeks burned and shined with fire within

Her rouge, bloody teardrops of the deprived
Her powder, the streaked white of weeping eyes

Her luck blackened by her thick twisting curls
Her sleep deranged by her brow's wispy curls

She'd lay down her tresses under her feet   565
She'd come and go like the early dawn breeze

To stay quiet was a difficult thing
To go roaming wild a difficult thing

Her opening in the game of disdain
Checkmated her in the chess match of pain

Like Venus she stayed up all the night long
The song of the harp was silent come dawn

At night she rolled up the carpet of youth
And kissed the threshold of Love's private room

Each night like a firefly on the road   570
She found her way to her fond desire's grove

And seeing her lover's eyes closed in sleep
She learned from the desperate moth how to weep

That nightingale sweetly singing her song
Moaned silently without making a sound

So gentle was every step that she took
Not even the sharpest thorn pierced her foot

She went on her way just like a fixed star
She seemed to turn with the heavens afar

She held her breath in the pain of her hurt   575
Trembling like a bubble yearning to burst

That great bird of fortune used to the light
Went like a blind bat who travels by night

Without fear she roamed the darkness unheard
As if she were meaning inside a word

She let fall her shadow cross the moonlight
So he would not feel the weight of its light

She wouldn't set foot on ground for the fear
Her shadow might fall and wake up her dear

She made shadow sculptures out of moonlight   580
And raised the arch of her sigh on the night

She'd not want to waken even her luck
It might shake her lover and wake him up

She came and went but she made not a sound
She seemed not to go beyond the heart's bound

Her grief-stricken heart mysteriously passed
All Zanzibar inside a looking glass

She lifted her veil and sighed at the sight
The sun of her face within black midnight

Her only desire was to see his face   585
And that he not be aware of her gaze

When she found her heart's caress was awake
She'd not open her book to desire's page

She soon made a friend of feverish pain
And tried to appear to laugh like a flame

With fairy tales sweetly told to entrap
She made up excuses why he should nap

In order to coax him gently to sleep
She'd tell of the squirrel's slumbering keep

She let her curls fall concealing her tears   590
And chattered about green meadows and meres

Her raving had for refrain a mad tune
That sung the tale of Leyla and Majnun

At last when that jasmine-faced boy would doze
Her eyes wandered like gazelles in that grove

She took a page, wise girl, from Majnun's book
Contenting herself with only a look

In this there is meaning clear manifest
For Beauty fell first in love with Love, yes

But choosing by night her love to admire   595
She kept aloof while abreast of desire

Spring

Ridvan who guards creation's paradise
The man pictured in the eyes of the wise

That is, the pen dressed up in its black robe
Begins in this way its speech to unfold:

When Spring who illuminates all the world
Bestowed its cup of New Year on the world

In surfeit of wine Time drunkenly fell
And broke the enchantment of its own spell

The music of joy filled all creation   600
Strange images rose in resurrection

Like heaven green fields in wave upon wave
Where roses and tulips drank in a daze

In each corner bloomed a spring of turquoise
Where flowers donned New Year's robes and rejoiced

I don't know what wine the sun had served up
The meadow's brood drank deep from Jamshid's cup

Pure wine poured down earthward instead of rain
And set all awhirl the green meadow's brain

Light puffy new clouds grazed there like gazelles   605
Drank hyacinth air and nourished themselves

The air was so moist, the weather so wet
Alongside the stream the breeze fell in step

Carnation received grace from the cloud mist
While rose rained perfume down on hyacinth

An emerald spring gushed forth upon high
Reflecting the emerald dome of the sky

The lightning cracked forth with laugher so sweet
The moon took to swearing oaths at its feet

The moon stretched out with its long milky beams   610
And scrambled up mercury with silver streams

The fog made men's mood so languid and deep
They buzzed like bees round the honey of sleep

The air gave such grace while sifting the rose
Rose-jam colocynths sprang up in the grove

Uproarious Spring with pleasure laughed loud
And strung the *tambur* with veins from a cloud

A moisture so heavy reigned in the air
The bird of flame could not fly anywhere

So wet in this weather's narcissus gaze   615
Could ever the rose's blush fly away?

The air with its falcon breast opened wide
Who was there could let the bird of sleep fly?

A wine full of madness struck vineyard's brain
Its foot was tied to the stream by a chain

New Year filled the air with moisture of spring
Each blade of grass was a parrot's green wing

The vulture of heaven swooped down to nest
The phoenix lay in a rosebud to rest

Such potency reached the flourishing of growth   620
Men's souls envied sapling trees in their growth

Grape clusters lay cradled in heaven's bower
And reached for a cloud's nipple in the shower

Each time that a cloud let fall pearly dew
It cheered all the laughing gay meadow's brood

The clouds made the orchard guard their sweet cache
The bee-parrots buzzed in that sugar cache

The vineyard took musk scent from the sweet breeze
The Erguvan's nosebleed would never cease

The rings of insanity linked in chains   625
The streams were mixed up with roses in waves

The torrent of April boisterously flowed
A pearl spun out of each fragment and stone

The world all eyes like a censer of glass
Each spring was a pretty rose-water flask

The whirling sky smoothed perfume on its mind
The flashes of lightning sneezed double time

Such thriving and growth came down to the ground
It flourished as high as heaven's fourth round

Each hill veined with rubies like Badakhshan   630
To vineyards the streams of rubies flowed down

Amidst such fertility rock and stone
Like rose-colored silk stuff shimmered and shone

Each bud flowering in the rose garden there
The secrets of earth and heaven laid bare

Rose branches became the antlers of bucks
Sweet cypresses gave the perfume of musk

The rose beds brought tidings from paradise
The Tuba tree rivaled there by mere vines

The sweet breezes blew Israfil's trumpet   635
To raise earth's crowd on the Day of Judgment

The heart's ardor swelled like a nightingale
As rosebud to rose related its tale

Waves of violets sprang up everywhere
The pen fell silent, the paper was bare

The narcissus discoursed on flute and wine
And scattered his pearls of speech on Kay's crown

In protest the plane tree raised up its hand
And held forth to make some fiery demand

The tulip lit its black wound with those words   640
The rose's lamp was shocked by what it heard

All heaven and earth filled with groans and tears
All that was said never did become clear

The daisies were painted like jasmine flowers
Blood dripped down the white cheeks of jasmine flowers

In secrecy rose and carnation kissed
Hyacinth waved to the grave narcissus

A whispering from the rose bed arose
And all to the gentle breeze was disclosed

Morning

A morning breeze brought the garden to life   645
The work of the dawn brought spiritual life

Dawn on the horizon was *Mary's palm*
Although sweet-breathed Christ was already born

The sun in epiphany rose so high
It seemed Moses had climbed up Mount Sinai

The sun filled the morn with glorious rays
Upon Crystal Mount Ali took his place

The jails and the dungeons opened their doors
In Egypt Joseph was sultan once more

The full moon lay down dawn's foundation stone   650
While Solomon gazed on Queen Sheba's throne

Hayder unsheathed Zulfikar there once more
And conquered Hayber again by the sword

The laughing dawn was the home of the sun
An Adam came to the garden again

The road to the unseen opened by Hizir
The world was the mirror of Alexander

Zamzam well took Ismail's sun as guest
He kissed his foot and showered him with gifts

In heart-rending morn the sun was in place   655
For Abraham fire by garden replaced

The sun shred the dawn from colored wool wisps
The parts of time were decked out with roses

The *stream of milk* flowed as Shirin looked up
And served lovers with her ruby-red cup

The face of the loved one finally appeared
But Jacob's eyes had gone blind from his tears

Beauty and Love Go Out to View the Pleasure Place of Meaning

Glorious Love was swayed by the weather
The eyes of his passion danced with pleasure

And Beauty's mood too took a different way   660
The two resolved on amusement and play

Those two shining candles set out and chose
The Pleasure Place of Meaning for abode

That Pleasure Place where there were to be found
Streams of violet and ambergris ground

That garden of paradise, that laughing earth
Was clay, but the clay of Adam's own birth

Each young sapling there was a Sidre tree
Each raw plum a heaven of olivine

The flourishing grass was eternal life   665
Its buds were suns and its dew, stars by night

The rose garden was a sea of red light
Rubies fit for sultans, pearls of pure light

A hundred Sinais of epiphany
Those hills never heard *You shall not see me*

Its bright lamps were revelation divine
With Gabriel's wing the meadows were lined

Faith's *lamp of night*, night flowers of the soul
Its autumn rose petals, essence of soul

Its jonquils the wealth of ocean and mine   670
Its narcissus, souvenir of paradise

The sun was a tree that shed light of dawn
The bird of the spirit there made its home

Each tree leaf there was an archangel's wing
Like blooms of the pomegranate rose-pink

A Kashmiri shawl with rosebuds on green
Was trite likeness for the blooms on that green

The guard at the vineyard gate there was Mars
He tended full moons instead of sunflowers

The apples, the oranges, fruit-bearing trees   675
Carnelian and coral red treasuries

The plain of the steppe was decked out with stars
And diamonds more numerous than dry stone shards

Strewn there in the dirt each fragment of stone
A star guiding lovers faithfully home

The Jesus rose never failing to tend
The flowers there were Mary's cyclamen

So many fresh downy-cheeked beauties there
The plains, steppes, sprung violets everywhere

Like thought's garden of fantastical things   680
For rosebuds nightingales bloomed with red wings

The Hizir of the grass an emerald sea
Peridot ships were rows of shrubbery

Like pistachio trees with branches hung down
Houris with their eyelashes swept the ground

The lamp of the rose there shining so fine
Burned brilliantly with the oil of red wine

Majnun's willow shook down its curly mane
Till Leyla took up the wild desert's chain

The cypress displayed its lofty physique   685
Resurrection Day fell down at its feet

The red poppy drunk on lunatic wine
Disdained goblets blown of crystal most fine

The Erguvan tree's fresh young sprouted shoots
Were bearing new fruit of the fire of youth

The vines were like polo sticks set with pearls
That bowed to the ground low like halberdiers

Black grapes, Hindus on the roof standing guard
But these stood watch on the roof of the stars

As everyone knows, the pink-and-white peach   690
Is soft as a pretty girl's lovely cheek

The succulent pear, fragrant, much preferred
Brought water by hand to cool the orchard

The tulips resplendent waved end to end
Like gardeners with royal red diadems

The plum trees were like luxuriance of fun
Each parrot-fruit chattered there on and on

The apricots, Leyla's ruby-red lips
Goblets of red wine were mad for a glimpse

The cherries were earrings set with garnet   695
The sight of them brought lovers' looks surfeit

Each blade of grass was a Kashmiri spring
Without change of season like a painting

Without like or number, bewitching eyes
Grazed like deer in that violet paradise

Black plums like the spring of life eternal
Or jewels of Ceylon that have no equal

Hyacinths framed the cheek of a wild rose
Carnations for those wild curls served as combs

The falcons there were not trained to the hunt   700
It was the peacock who tracked the pheasant

The *hoopoes* like Jam wore crowns on their heads
The fairy troops francolin and partridge

That garden of wild and untended flame
Regarded the sun and moon with disdain

Hearts burning made fireworks burst in the skies
Enlightened hearts winked there like fireflies

The Pool of Grace

A blessed pool watered that noble place
It was known by name as the Pool of Grace

The Lord kept that heavenly water refreshed   705
With liquid of silver oft replenished

Without doubt that deep pool of clarity
Was mirror to witness of mystery

Secreted therein were myriad aspects
A sea of qualities, pearl of essence

Each clam there concealed a treasure of light
Half closed like the lids of houri eyes bright

Each moment the silver mirror of that pool
Displayed the image of another world

Hizir's fountain flooded that pristine mound   710
Made greenery flourish on noble ground

Wine pure of fault came to that fountain spring
And envy transformed it to a fire spring

The whirling sky drowned there, dazzled and pale
Moon and sun were there Jonah and the whale

In view of that water heaven's Tesnim
Would bow like a beggar groveling in shame

That garden so gaily blooming, in short
Was like to the talent of a pure poet

On the Wonders of Poetry, Manservant at the Pleasure Place of Meaning

A sage young at heart and sprightly of limb   715
At that pleasing garden welcomed guests in

70

By name Poetry, his essence most dear
Was prior to every heavenly sphere

Love and Beauty's natures he knew of old
And properties special to warmth and cold

His thought a night lamp of knowledge divine
Cognizant of lover's and beloved's mind

Himself both the question and the answer
Miracle of prophecy and messenger

Unrivaled in guiding right or astray   720
Confinement and freedom under his sway

He could if he chose without shield or sword
Make peace raid the caravan of dread war

He would, when he was indulgent and kind,
Make lover and beloved of death and life

Now he was a demon, now a naiad
Now swam in the sea, now walked on the land

The road's Hizir to those lost on the way
A shah to the friendless and the afraid

Now he was a poet, now doctor of law   725
Now sorcerer, now a strict man of God

Joy and despair both doomed by his decree
Hope and desire quailed at his tyranny

71

There flowed every moment at his command
Both tears of the grieved and tears of the glad

He made those in sorrow happy and pleased
He made the sharp-witted languid with sleep

The qualities of his mind can't be told
It held meanings to all others unknown

Each and every creature depends on him   730
All that is not finds existence through him

He made the beauty of the moon-faced shine
And he was the ashes on pining eyes

A boon companion for the content
A robe of mourning for those in torment

He gave comfort as required by the care
Appeared in the mirror as required there

Without effort, when considering it fit,
He made a thing cause its own opposite

Now like Joseph jailed in the pit of gloom   735
Now prized in the Egypt of great fortune

For Poetry's honor this share is vile
In number his qualities exceed lies

Digression

O ye who seek meaning's luminous jewel
Give ear to my speech with attention due

In this regard there are certain aspects
Discussion of which gives cause to digress

Some lunatics dressed as rational men
Claim new poetry has come to an end

As if the great poets of olden days   740
All borrowed from those of their olden days

In no man is there still worthiness left
The business of poets must then be theft

"Is there anything that has not been said?
One single thing that has been left unsaid?"

While this is not worthy of a reply
Of pearls of address spent to give the lie

Still there are a few who jabber like jinn
Dregs left by a tribe of Jinn son of Jinn

Who call themselves the great poets of the age   745
And bow on the prayer mat of the café

They babble on in their ill-omened snooze
Consumed in their own fires like the Kaknus

They bow and cow to each other and say:
"That's how it is, gentlemen, I daresay

Where now that great poet, sage of the West
Broomsweep Softy, may he slumber in peace

And then there's Tormented, suffering's sigh
Ayni Chelebi, that light of the eye

They've gone and took poetry with them, alas   750
We here are left spared by the sword, alas

Let our worth be appreciated, friends
Men of genius will not be seen again"

In order to sell their poetry now
They deny originality now

Inkpots on their belts, their verses in hand
In the shops, in the streets, much in demand

They wag their heads, say as if in a pique
"Ah, oh for Sabit—now he was unique"

Since their own talents are ever so slight   755
They'd like to make verse's dawn a dark night

Conclusion

Then dilettante scribblers among the scribes
Who mostly are senior clerks among scribes

Those billowing cloaks of smug vanity
Who stir up the sea of terminology

To their minds the ultimate in fine art
Would be to learn Ragib's *Writings* by heart

A couple of young boys to pass the time
A volume of verse, music and some wine

If one should to hard work feel disinclined   760
From these it is that strength is to be mined

Does not this define the word "catamite"?
Is not poethood thus tasteless and trite?

No poets come from the seminary crowd
No, I will not even speak of that crowd

With quotes from *The Summary* mollas make
Pretensions to verse—their pretexts are fake

And here in our city more friends than should
Rush frantically off to art's neighborhood

They take lessons with Ashik Turani   765
All secondhand, borrowed from Revani

Like flies picking up false rumors and worse
They try to contemn the honey of verse

In sum then, original poetry
Scarce as a well-balanced talent must be

The First Argument: On the Existence of Poetry

O ye who know subtleties of pure sense
Give ear to the discourse of this swift pen

Though we scrutinize the surface of things
God's names and *sites manifest* are like twins

Prior in existence to death and life   770
Munificent God was quickener of life

But joined to each other in succession
Are creator, creature, and creation

Each instant *divine names* step into view
And set spinning heaven's wheel of fortune

Impute to God's self no contrarieties
All effects proceed from God's qualities

Thus order and change could not be for naught
In each attribute of God's there is cause

God the Truth is prior, without flaw or cease   775
Without tongue or voice, God the Truth speaks

Things empowered need one to empower them
There's one who causes speech to be spoken

It's God the Truth who showers forth poetry
Humankind is the site of this bounty

If you know the one who said *"will not fail ..."*
Reject the phantom Mutazilite error

There can be no bound to God's qualities
The blessing of poetry cannot cease

Give this matter consideration due   780
Could our forebears have exhausted that boon?

Beyond bound, estimate, analogy
New poetry is uttered constantly

May you find the power to comprehend
Let me have my say now and you attend

Is not *perpetual creation*, above all
Of original poetry the true cause?

The Second Argument: On the Necessity of Poetry

Before Islam, in times of ignorance
All the world vied in claims to eloquence

The fair at Ukaz was set up each year   785
And poetry competitions held there

With sword and tongue they staked their pretensions
Duels went in hand with improvisations

But when the one living, ever-praised Lord
By bestowing the Koran on the world

Made miracle with eloquence coincide
The eloquent tribesmen were terrified

So those wayward tribes should come to know awe
Produce its parallel—*thus proposed God*

Still unparalleled stands that miracle   790
The word of the living, the powerful

If men lost the power to judge and reflect
That challenge, that miracle, would lose effect

If all eloquence and poetry ceased
The Koran's virtue could not be perceived

If no poet could compose poetry
God's proof would inadequate prove to be

He made it to show man's powerlessness
But could God's empowering be powerless?

I've dismissed my foes with manifest proof   795
I've tested my talent by Koran's proof

The Third Argument: On the
Universality of the Necessity

Abu Hanife, chief of imams wise
Did not deem the Arabic prayer obliged

He favored miracle's universality
He ruled for the meaning's necessity

In explication he said furthermore
Though his reverse ruling is the stronger

That peoples not Arab may be allowed
To use their own language praying to God

In every age poets, surely a few   800
Declare the *incomparability* too

Expending their share of pure imagery
They tender their awe with their poetry

On the Nature of Poethood

To say poet is to say man of heart
A tolerant man and gentle of heart

Or shall a whole army of vile scoundrels
Who eat crumbs from whispering Satan's table

Drink freely the cup of style's libation?
Should they befriend the heart's inspiration?

Poethood requires a burning desire   805
Attended by anxiety and trial

He'll condescend neither to lip nor cheek
In his garden blooms a rose not-yet-seen

He searches down each and every path well
His imagery's falcon captures gazelle

Once inside imagination's steep way
He'll not run across the demon hearsay

If matters lead to learned argument
His pen must be informed in argument

In the sea of wine let his thought dive deep   810
It's the man with a pearl I wish to see

What I call a pearl is not that trite phrase
Juxtaposing "eye" and "brow" in one place

Strutting with pretensions like barnyard fowl
One egg laid, a thousand boastings and scowls

Obscure, Arabic vocabulary
Gross, grosser and grossest as it can be

"Look here, what a sweet style, oh my, what bliss!
A sipping ruby beside a rose kiss!

Mark the *association* in this verse   815
'A dark night of exile and dark black curls'

The word 'dagger,' mark his delicacy now
He's made an allusion to her eyebrow!"

This too demonstrates considerable art
But poetry is something much apart

A poet of wit and temperament pure
Once spoke this herein appropriate verse:

"Don't touch any phrase that's been so chewed over
As to have been said even once before"

Since we are inclined to elusive style   820
We speak in a fresh, original style

Not contrived conceit, not false subtlety
Weighed down with claims to superiority

Is verse so-called science, jabber and guff?
Or shall I not speak—oh come now, be just

Conclusion

They found poetry lofty in renown
Nizami and Ferdowsi and Khusraw

In Nevai's style Fuzuli attained
The path reaching poetry's high domain

Here in our Istanbul Nevizade   825
Gave chase, but in his pedestrian way

Should his verse be peer to Nizami's song?
Are Gypsy harps music for the Koran?

His talent, it's true, cannot be denied
And with him so many others have vied

For each of them shout a thousand bravos
Swear a thousand curses upon their foes

We're stealing poetry from poetry
Let us return now to our own story

Poetry Becomes Their Go-Between

When Poetry saw these two new to woe   830
He understood what they would undergo

Now he looked at Beauty's face carefully
Now he regarded Love attentively

Like apples the two were both of a piece
In countenance yellow, though red of cheek

To him their condition seemed quite perverse
It seemed this game had been played in reverse

Upon the two youths he took compassion
And played the role of go-between for them

In no way could he possibly accept   835
That Beauty could be Love's humble subject

How could one believe the light of the moon
Would transform *flax* into immortal morn?

His path of reflection was bare of thought
Could it ever be that torch burned for moth?

The signs of affection were very clear
Why try to foretell what's already there?

There was one thing he could not verify
From whom to whom was this urging and fire?

The tribe's ancient customs followed this truth: 840
The maiden should be courted by the youth

Thus was the established law of the land
No case of this kind had yet come to hand

Although it was true each ventured a gaze
One must be the falcon, the other prey

Her heart like her curls was crushed underfoot
Love tossed her not even the slightest look

He saw that these two rebellious upstarts
Had come up with some new way of the heart

For Beauty he felt compassion and said   845
Offering to her his support as a friend,

"Confide in me, come, let's talk in private
It's simple, if you don't complicate it

Since this court was founded so long ago
Solomon has had need of the *hoopoe*

For victory take a friend of the road
Find Shapur and be Khusrev of the world

One finds the beloved, finding the friend
Don't think of friend as a rival to friend

This point travelers of the path all maintain   850
Path and companion are one and the same

Those hastening hearts awake on this path
Once having found the friend, have found the path

He who goes alone, though he were the sun,
Will abide in blood until kingdom come

One finds the beloved finding the friend
The friend is the goal, if you comprehend"

And so in fact with the aid of that sage
Their fellowship was renewed day by day

Appeal and refusal, rehearsed in turn   855
Became milk and sugar in their converse

By heart's desire, each one for the other
Two moons became each other's customer

But what can be done, this commerce was snuffed
Cruel fortune thought such sweetness a bit much

I don't know what wind it was swept in strong
Rose withered and nightingale stopped his song

Call to the Saki

Come Saki, is this any time to stop?
Is this some kind of test? Come now, why stop?

O Saki, be gracious and rain down wine   860
Be a cloud, but rain rubies pure and fine

Don't sigh, this is just a bargain in trade
For one rose you get a thousand hells' trade

Crush one spark in the gash of my heart's wound
One teardrop, a thousand roses in bloom

Saki, is there not one drop of wine left?
I'm weeping blood, is there no kebab left?

Saki, bring wine from the Erguvan tree
I'm dry, it's the fire of youth has burned me

I'm hostage to exile, sick and distraught   865
Prescribe for the pulse the requisite draught

Has cruel fate's wheel now spun to an end?
Don't settle on stillness, turn round again

Since life is the patron of raucous haste
Drink faster and we'll outstrip its mad race

Come heighten the passion of fond desire
Let us explicate the grief of exile

Dazzle Appears and Forbids Their Fellowship

Majnun attired in his black mourning garb
That is, my pen, weak and troubled at heart

To Leyla, unfailing dream of his soul   870
Commences his secret thus to disclose

There once was a powerful man of the tribe
A lion named Dazzle whom none could try

Commanding that country from end to end
He took control also of those two friends

By destiny's spy he'd been made aware
Of feelings that Love and Beauty had shared

Surrounding all with his power like fate
He raised up a wall of severance strait

For these two, he said, it would not be wise   875
To gamble in glances unsupervised

It was a hard task to challenge his dictate
Those moons had no choice but to separate

Behold and see how cruel fortune's caprice
Will never allow two friends any peace

The mansion of Beauty's face was her tent
She'd been a moon, now she was forced to set

His majesty Love, that radiant sun
Was left to writhe in the blood light of dawn

Beauty's Fantasies

In Beauty's daydreams she pictured herself   880
In battle with Dazzle all by herself

She'd unsheathe a sigh to burn up the soul
And raze to the ground that foe's house and home

Poetry Advises Her

In an instant Poetry came to her aid
But he arrived in state of disarray

He started to give much counsel and said
"Don't make Dazzle target of your hatred

Your enmity here is quite out of place
That man is the mirror to your friend's face

Don't make your heart's sigh a drunken Negro   885
Don't shatter the mirror's glass of Love so"

When he had expounded all of his proofs
This much was the kernel he had produced

"To knock down that house would be a disgrace
Whose one wall looks toward your beloved's face

You write an epistle, I'll take it there
Then for a short while appear without care

Do not war with Dazzle, let go the past
So that Love may be pleased with you at last"

That ravishing girl, no recourse left her   890
Contented herself with writing a letter

Although from her pen words came in a flood
She wrote her epistle with tears of blood

Conforming to the advice she received
With this epistle her case she did plead

Beauty's Letter to Love

At my letter's head I write the Lord's name
The merciful, prior, alive, self-sustained

Who raises the skies up proud above earth
And measures out mercy from sky to earth

Who ruins the palace of fond desire   895
Who shatters the legs of hope gone awry

Who grants the desiring wishes fulfilled
Who grants to the poets fame and goodwill

Creator of good and evil from naught
For pious and libertine he solves knots

And many a salutation bestow
Upon him who intercedes for his folk

His chosen companions and family
Upon them all, salutations of peace

Let this letter reach the friend of my soul   900
It's but a sigh, to the skies let it go

Although the pain I feel can't be revealed
It cannot, no more than fire, be concealed

This letter a miserable pauper wrote
Is folded in two like her broken heart

The cruel tyrant I address is a shah
And my letter but dust in his regard

O Shah who grants friendship to his mere slave
What now is it has brought on your disdain?

I was the wretch you blessed with your regard   905
Who is it now, sir, that's captured your heart?

Although I know you don't stray far from me
You are not so faithless and could not be

Exile has exhausted all that I know
Do not the delirious rant and rave so?

It's sudden disaster has me in thrall
May God quickly bring an end to it all

My proud one, though I have stooped to entreat
I dwell in a cage—what choice is left me?

However a woman may wield the sword   910
Her tool of desire is not in accord

In those days when you and I breathed as one
I drank down the cup of passionate love

The way we were was clear for all to see
If you're a man don't you now neglect me

That feeling is lost and now I am weak
I ran wild and now I have broken wings

The pain of loss has arrived in this town
Want has arrived and fulfillment is gone

Lord Dazzle has blocked my union with you   915
Don't let a mere letter satisfy you

The law of protection would not approve
Of powerful men who powerless prove

Let us suppose I deserve no esteem
There's no doubt I'm dust at my lover's feet

But if the sun who all vast heaven rules
Fails to account for a dust mote, it's cruel

You feel no compassion for me, my love
Think, someday the resurrection will come

For many years I was your rose of spring   920
Now autumn has come and I am fading

With all my heart and soul I cherished you
And to the extent I could I served you

Now that I am in a difficult way
Have mercy, don't leave me weeping astray

You will hear no more persuasion from me
It will be my death or union, pay heed

I'll have satisfaction in union or
In death make my fame abide evermore

Lord Dazzle has made me wretched and weak   925
It falls to you to take action, my sweet

If you do have any interest in me
Come, let sighs and sad cries your custom be

The tribe surely will hear of your desire
And granting you union, silence your cry

If you are offended by what has passed
Do not torture me, beware of God's wrath

This trouble is not just something I've done
You have been unjust to me so often

O moon who paints black the luck of my star   930
Consider the vengeance of God, beware!

You too could encounter circumstance dire
You too, like my sigh, could be clothed in fire

Don't drive me to exile, helpless and hurt
At least give me some few comforting words

Give thanks to the Lord, my pure white jasmine
If I had been you, and you, I—what then?

If scandal of my disgrace offends you
Then show me the right way I should pursue

Can modesty rest in a lover's heart?   935
Can anyone do more than play his part?

I know for you there exists no such pain
But fortune does harbor swift winds of change

It's not clear what future fate will unveil
So many have unawares met this trial

The tribe's custom is as clear as can be
That you are the one who should esteem me

If ever the youth disdain his sworn bride
The girl stays at home and swallows her pride

Her sighing and moaning bring no recourse   940
The flood of her tears will not reach the shore

It's for me to burn and suffering withstand
The rest must come from you, you make a plan

O moon, here my words have come to an end
May God grant to them a favorable end

Poetry Brings the Letter to Love

The instant that speech had come to an end
The letter was passed to Poetry's hand

And Poetry sped in haste down the road
He went to the shah just like the *hoopoe*

Arriving, he found Love silent and mute   945
Dumbstruck as had been his wont all his youth

Nor heartache's hell nor delight in the end
As if there were neither rival nor friend

Said Poetry, "Come, enough of this mood
Now open the letter, read your fortune

Look how peerless Beauty, her majesty
Has distanced herself from you severely

She moans in despair thousandfold laments
And tells a tale of the word severance"

When Love heard this he regained his good sense   950
Then fell in a swoon and lost consciousness

He lay dead to self there for a long time
And then when he spoke, blood flowed from his eye

He asked him, "What kind of letter is that?
Show me, what black robe of mourning is that?"

He glanced at the letter from head to foot
And soon the gist of it all understood

He took pen in hand and wrote straightaway
A letter in answer without delay

Love's Letter to Beauty

In heading, the name of the glorified   955
Who created soul and brought forth the mind

Who tends to the flourishing realm of trial
Who severs two loving friends with exile

Who fashions of Beauty a radiant sun
And makes meat of Love to roast thereupon

Who gives the despairing hope of union
Who makes lovers slaves of deprivation

And many a prayer for God's messenger
And Betul, great Shah of Shahs, his daughter

And let many salutations of peace   960
His children and all his family reach

This letter is black, a smoldering spark
The ashes left from the flames of my heart

I write to a heaven where those who dwell
Take rest in the springtime flowers of hell

The living are those with power to speak
But sometimes the world can make the dead speak

O sovereign who puts to death her own slave
Plan? What is that? What recourse do I have?

Your letter has reached my miserable heart   965
The arrow was shot and wounded its mark

That story contained I don't know what spell
It brought to my soul the tidings of hell

This thing I call hell has no recompense
There's one word inside it, called severance

For all the long time I was dumb and deaf
So fearful it made me sick unto death

Since you didn't see that I was aware
You thought that you loved and I did not care

And I, when I now think back on those days   970
I realize that my heart was amazed

I'm helpless, what is this force that you have
Good God, but your patience has run out fast

O Shah who thinks she herself is in thrall
It's Joseph who was thrown down in the well

The henna upon your hand is not blood
Zuleyha possesses no share of love

O rose, do not say you're bleeding and pale
Don't think me a weak and frail nightingale

What you think is blood is just rouge, at most   975
The nightingale's song does not charm the rose

Don't think you're the ruin of pain and blight
You are the resplendent sun of daylight

It's I who am plagued by thousandfold grief
And I have a universe for each grief

You saw me in patience suffering defy
And thought that I had the power to fly

When you, alas, heard the nightingale's song
You thought that the moth was guilty of wrong

Although on this path there is gain in store   980
The ocean of heartache has no far shore

But on this one judgment lovers agree
Pain must be in secret borne, secretly

Since you wish to make it publicly known
The cure for lament is easily shown

If love's quarrel is the claim you invoke
Here cruel heaven and here my sigh of smoke

From now on it's idol worship for me
The life ascetic and drunk ecstasy

Could it ever be, once you have said "cry!"   985
That any flood could daunt my weeping eye?

If you want me to do what must be done
Don't ever tire of my cries from now on

No mark had been made in heartache's ledger
I had from you yet no hope of pleasure

I'd put that desire aside out of view
And now it seems there's work for me to do

The command is yours and so is the fruit
Self-sacrifice, mine, the rest up to you

Behold all that grief and suffering can be   990
How judgment will from my suit now proceed

I doubt my soul would take oath in bad faith
I'll not break my word, come Resurrection Day

This here is the plan that I have conceived
Be gay, my sad-eyed girl, do not be grieved

The lords of the tribe are just this and that
Let them withdraw, it's life-or-death combat

Who is there who'd dare to bar my progress?
My soul is my meat and God my witness

Be patient and watch a while, do not cry   995
Let's see what almighty God will provide

Guard this letter as you would your life, please
And that vow you made ... have mercy on me!

Mistress Modesty, Beauty's Nurse

When she was kept far from Love's countenance
Painful thoughts made Beauty anxious and tense

Her nurse, the firebrand Mistress Modesty
Had dandled that candle upon her knee

At first to her rose she'd but milk allow
Then drops of dew with the sweat of her brow

She had in the season of the dawn breeze   1000
Tempered her in the stream of modesty

Now hearing her cry alone in her room
She sensed Beauty's grief and fell in a swoon

The reed shoot of severance rose past the veil
As carefully Modesty listened well

She sensed that her little moon-fragment one
Was longing to be the star to a sun

She knew not what kind of pain hers might be
For what rose these cold sighs of hers might be

Each night when she gazed on her heart's caress   1005
The wound in her heart was branded afresh

As Beauty's heart burned with marks of distress
This one made a wick of her curling tress

When she stood tall as a cypress and sighed
Judgment Day broke loose within this one's mind

As Beauty let her tears flow to sea
She'd head for the desert miserably

With every breath Beauty heaved a deep sigh
No one but the Lord and Love could know why

When Modesty asked her why did she hurt   1010
A chilly sigh was the answer she heard

Then Beauty recounted what had occurred
Interpreting her dream in her own words

"There is no recourse, I've met my downfall
Alone I am wandering in Kerbala

My soul is a peddler of regret's jewel
My eyes drink the brimming cup full of rue

The glass of my heart is shattered with loss
The moonlight has gone and left but a gloss

I'm set adrift on a sea without shore   1015
Without a fortress I'm fighting a war

My heart's enemy is bad luck most foul
Behold here a ruin shunned by the *owl*

Dark night hides the beauty of my friend's face
The mirror reflects chagrin in his place

The stars have disordered my happy life
The wound in my heart is my cup of life

A lightning bolt came to strike and destroy
It left all in ruin my house of joy

I'm kept hostage to the pain of exile   1020
My rival enjoys my lover meanwhile

The mouth of the bud is dumb and amazed
A dewdrop fell on the flower of flame

I'm friendless, the task before me severe
God merciful, bountiful, veil my fear

I am deranged by the curls of his brow
And now is revealed the writ on my brow

I'm sick in exile while he is carefree
It hurts that he doesn't care to cure me

I've no leave to even cry out in pain   1025
Though anticipation is a great bane

If I loose my fiery crocodile sigh
That rebel will turn on me by and by

My eye is the moist tear shed by the rose
Expectation's cup will yet overflow

I drift in pain's vessel without recourse
My friends and rescuers cry on the shore

There's no one of whom I've the slightest need
My medicine has no power to cure me

The ghouls of despair strike on my king's road   1030
My mind and my judgment have fled back home

I'm naught but a passion all on my own
Of whom to whom should I then cry and moan?

I've fallen a prey to grief, hear my plea
There's none I can blame for this tyranny

My dearest has found the sector of faith
If only I could be lost in that place

Had my heart recourse for wandering astray
It would be no less than salvation's way

Surely Hizir would come if he knew how   1035
If he does exist, he must be lost now

I've fallen sick in the hands of my foes
I was precious crystal, now I am broke

The flowers of my face are stolen away
I have need of yet another spring day

My tresses and curls all stab and sting me
The scorpion in my tomb torments me

In heaving a sigh I'm like a long lance
I'm swallowed up by the snake of my glance

My slim form, compared to a ruby wand   1040
Is now the dead bridegroom's funeral frond

My ruby lips languish as my eyes did
In speech's sweet draught death's poison is hid

The flame of my cheek has set me on fire
My springtime is now all blood in my eye

My eyes sewn fast to expectation's road
My lashes are fairies at springs of blood

The rose of my passion never did bloom
My heedless sleep like a nightingale flown

I'm so confused that the world seems to be   1045
Filled all with blood, poison, and savagery

Lightning surrounds me, I feel such alarm
To me hell itself is a babe in arms

The prospect of happiness brings me such fear
I'd suffer if you said be of good cheer

Hellfire in my eyes is sunlight of morn
While heaven sticks in my eye like a thorn"

That orb of the sun with such brilliant rays
Sank deep in this sea of hurt and dismay

She stirred up a flood of worries and fears   1050
And wept oceans upon oceans of tears

Like teardrops she seeped down into the ground
And heaved like a sigh that rose heaven-bound

"Don't bother the lovesick, asking questions
Don't rile up the soldier with suggestions

It's judgment of fate has befallen me
God only knows what has happened to me

Can pain be explained to one free of care?
More than anything, it's beyond compare

Don't ask the wild moth about his desire   1055
Know passion by how he burns in the fire

If I'd known about this striving and war
I would not have plundered fortitude's floor

Would you be so kind as not to insist
The fire in my soul should fall on my lips?

Cruel fate has enslaved me, chained in exile
It's slaked even thirsty me with exile

While I sigh and cry alone and shut in
Don't you be unjust too and listen in

It's dangerous, you will be destroyed too   1060
The shaft of my sigh will stab and wound you

While you measure out the length of my sighs
The road to disgrace looms before your eyes

From now on I'll be famed throughout the land
With each day in pain I'm less in command

The hearth of my breast is ruined past repair
I'm cooked in this passion, hear my despair

This longing belongs to misery's Kaaba
For prayers groans are heaved in that House of God

They pray to the doctor to make them ill   1065
They suffer and wish to suffer more still

All those who resolve to travel this path
Find safety with bandits crossing their path

Come, be my companion, don't contemn me
Do you know the high road to infamy?

When lover and beloved part in pain
What difference could modesty make or shame?

My lover has sacrificed this my life
Will that not suffice for trial in this life?"

Modesty Becomes Aware of Beauty's Wretchedness

When nurse Mistress Modesty heard this news   1070
Her torment outstretched her solicitude

She wished that she never had begged to hear
With frustration's fist she beat lip and ear

"Alas, but I've fallen deep into care
It was I who asked, and now I'm aware

With this one spark I have razed hearth and home
If only I could have left things alone!

Had my ears and eyes but been deaf and blind
My pleasure in life would not be defiled

Now here is this trouble, prospects are bleak   1075
The illness is fatal, the patient weak

It's plain as can be this is pain of Love
This girl is awhirl on the path of Love

'Beloved,' she thought and, silenced in shame,
Immediately she forgot Love's name

Is there anything that might be obscure?
Without Love could such grief ever endure?"

But this darling had to be comforted
This flower had to be cultivated

Contriving advice as best she could   1080
She started her discourse on chaste girlhood

Modesty Argues with Beauty

"O rose of my fond desire," she said
"Bloom flowering fresh in my heart's rose bed

For every disease there is, there's a cure
For each patient there is health, to be sure

Don't make it your wont to tell tales, my dove
You've fallen, but still, don't cry out to Love

Observe utmost care, my girl like a rose
These things you've said, don't let lip or tongue know

Do not allow your laments to increase   1085
Don't lose honor and good name to caprice

One word from the lips that has skyward flown
Should not in a thousand ears settle down

That secret you do not steadfastly keep
Will not within one breast peacefully sleep

Mystery is a great shah, honor him well
Don't cast him outdoors, entertain him well

Or one day the army, when all is known
Will turn upside-down both you and your home

Attend to advice, be kind and astute   1090
Don't ever tell secrets, be resolute

Take on every color but give no tint
Don't tarnish the mirror of innocence

A word is like lightning, hearts are haystacks
It leaves its spark and can't be taken back

A word is a target while it ascends
And razes the ground on which it descends

It's due to the words shot by the taut bow
That it finds no respite from groaning low

You'll publish your secret for all to hear   1095
You'll act in haste and impatience, I fear"

Beauty Answers Modesty

When Beauty heard this speech troubled and grieved
She wept poison tears and laughed bitterly

She said, "You do practice uncommon skill
You would have a rushing torrent be still

Could I renounce Love? Could such a thing be?
It's clear you have never understood me

You don't know the cure, so don't ask this time
Don't tire out the patient with nursery rhymes

I thought you would speak the language of Love   1100
That you would bring miserable me news of Love

But you dropped that subject quick as you please
And spoke about mirrors and mysteries

The sky has grown tight round my head, I say!
Is there need for Plato's barrel today?

What thing is honor, what word is troth?
Why talk about mummies with a wild moth?

I flee toward the fire raging ahead
And you tell me there is danger ahead

About shahs and armies you lecture me   1105
And say not to tarnish my purity

What wine is it that intoxicates me?
What thing is it that you now forbid me?

If it's fairy tales that you want to hear
You listen and I'll recite to you, dear"

Then rising up like the sea in a squall
"O Love!" she cried out and would say no more

Modesty Comes Up with Another Pretext

Peerless Modesty saw Beauty was vexed
And tried again with a different pretext

"His majesty matchless Love," she began   1110
"Is fearless and strong, a very brave man

At school you and he do share the same desk
The tribe stands together in this respect

There is no doubt you've been promised to him
You will taste eternal union with him

But he will not find this business approved
To have you pursuing, and he pursued

And then, if such talk should spread far and wide
Won't he find the scandal hard to abide?

Although you desire him, be without tongue   1115
Be grave, you're a maid, not easily won

My fear is if Master Love hears the news
He'll practice with Rivalry's sword on you"

Beauty Thinks of Something Else

Beauty made her mind a sheath for these words
For she'd spoken "Love" with each single word

"Dear life, what is death if not life," she cried
"While yet hope of my beloved abide!

I fear that my love may grow tired of me
While you fear that he may do harm to me

So sickly was I, bewildered and blind   1120
This blunder of speech had quite slipped my mind

You've made me aware without meaning to
You moaned and I thought I heard you say 'moon'

My lips will be sealed though my heart is squeezed
May only that rose not wither in pique

Let me choke on blood, I'll not make it known
So strangers may not rub salt in his wound

This soul fearlessly will burn and be true
If only he won't shoot one glance of rue

From now on in silence will I remain   1125
Though I should die I will not speak his name

How do you chastise me, almighty God
To burn in the fire and still not cry out"

Modesty Blocks the Road of Complaint

Said Modesty, "There's no cure for such care
May God teach that love of yours to be fair

That bright moon is filled with rage when you sigh
His eyes will grow dark if ever you cry

'It's mine to cry out and moan,' he will say
'And for my beloved to steadfast stay'"

Beauty Is Silent

So Beauty took heed, and with much regret   1130
Made firm her resolve to play hard to get

Her place was the corner, like a *kanun*
All others could see was that she withdrew

Poetry Brings the Information to Love

In order to comprehend this affair
In secrecy Poetry was hid there

He overheard everything that was said
He listened all through unbeknownst to them

When Poetry was thus fully informed
He left and went to make Love too informed

He said, "Beauty's heart is burning for you   1135
Now give justice, you heart kindler, as due

Is it fit that Beauty should wail and cry
While you do not make your soul sacrifice?

By God, is the game of love played like this?
The beloved made to beg for a kiss?

From now on look to increase your desire
Accustom yourself to pain of exile"

The Reversal of Events: Love Goes Mad with Desire for Beauty

We now come upon unsatisfied Love
That lion-born weakling, sickly boy Love

In private he lit his breast-searing sighs   1140
And idled away his days a few nights

He kept safe his camphor from every spark
As with the dawn's wick he lit up the dark

That is, the bright vision of his love's face
Made night stay up late to visit daybreak

When anxious thoughts bound him fast in a chain
He'd give the dream of her tresses free rein

When wine he imbibed made drunk ardor slip
He silenced and shut his salt ruby lip

Afloat on grief's sea, he lost his own name   1145
And came to rest calling out Beauty's name

The trick of a promise hid from the eyes
Made of his hope's grove lemon paradise

In sum, raucous Love had all this time been
Full of joy in hope of union to win

But when it was said that they two must part
The needle of severance broke in his heart

His delicate form and visage of light
Was like the *man of the eye* weakly bright

He didn't know fortune's wheel of discord   1150
Would part them with one sharp note of discord

The daybreak of union happily won
He didn't foresee its night was to come

He saw his beloved as his true friend
And thought fortune's play could have any end

Is not the disdain of one's lover worth
All pleasures bestowed on heaven and earth?

And if the beloved should importune,
The lover in hell finds his honeymoon

Can such joy by any means be endured   1155
Whose one instant is more dear than the world?

And then separation comes as a trial
Few lovers there are who'll gird for that trial

Who can from the very start of love's game
Make passion arise from chilly disdain?

Who is there can stand such ghastly demise
Thrown into hell out of sweet paradise?

It seems the beloved wanted it so
The poor boy had snakebite for antidote

The hunter a thousand times chants his verse   1160
A thousand times *Perished be* . . . in reverse

But once the gazelle is caught in his net
He raises his cruel sword without regret

Unhappiness is not ever concise
It can't be divided and summarized

Shall words and discourse encompass those sighs?
One spear like that won't fit inside the sky

A world of sparks burns in one grieving heart
That star isn't found on any sky chart

What meaning have words in this sea of woe?   1165
This fire has the power to bring heaven low

When Love feared that Beauty had said farewell
The hand of remorse ripped out with a yell

He wept jeweled tears more than thousandfold
And crushed diamonds in the wound of his soul

He couldn't speak he was in such a daze
And couldn't be silent, he was so crazed

There was in his heart but pain of desire
There was in his eye nor flood nor the fire

His broken heart poured out through eyes that   1170
    bled
Fire streamed out with every word that he said

He blew on the sea of deep discontent
Its froth rose beyond the sky's vast extent

So cold was the sigh that he heaved in hell
He made the dark night of cruel winter yell

The more that he craved her, crying, Oh, ah!
December became July, and cold, hot

Sometimes when he'd face the sun and grumble
He raged like a fire in front of a bubble

At times gazing at the stars in the skies   1175
He'd raze heaven's crop with lightning-bolt sighs

He'd not roam the wild like Majnun distraught
He looked at a city and made it naught

The glittering tears he shed so ran on
The world became all mirage and maelstrom

He wasted away, a thread of mere sparks
He drew toward the land of naught a faint arc

He was a mosquito, scorned and minute
And made heaven's Nimrod out for a dupe

That moon was so starved and thin he could ride   1180
As traveling companion fit for a sigh

But still, in his perfect magnificence
He shook the divine throne with reverence

Let Love sigh for Beauty, deep in misery
If the world collapse, then so let it be!

That breast doubled over with a crushed heart
What does it care if the world falls apart?

If sky should convulse and fall, what of it?
If only it please the lady beloved

Quick Love had now slipped out from in between   1185
If heaven and earth burned, what did that mean?

Since none find the comfort there they expect
The ark of the sky deserves a shipwreck

Sometimes when he felt most deeply depressed
He'd write verse like this in rhyming quintets

Lyric

The shah who has made a slave of my heart
Keeps murderous fiends for her bodyguard
Her glance and her ruby speak with one heart
Bloodthirsty is her look of disregard
Her arrow of pain well knows the soul's way   1190

Her court of fate's built on justice awry
Her hangmen are trembling souls, terrified
Shouts for justice are heard from every side
The brawl of doomsday, laments and deep sighs
Is this Kerbala here or Judgment Day?

The jewel of her lips is Noah unseen
Her eye harbors spiritual life unseen
The blood that she sheds is the wine unseen
The grace of her speech is victory unseen
Her each word is life and won't fade away   1195

If she sends her curls to plunder and raid
Apostasy grips the soldiers of faith
It's fear of this makes her tresses deranged
Her murderous sword is proof of her claim
Alas, the affair is weirdly astray

Let my helpless heart ever burn and grieve
Let only that goddess of fire believe
Let my soul in blood of exile dive deep
Let her languid eye drink wine to surfeit
When she's in a rage a thousand souls pay   1200

Like Galib a hundred thousand in love
Drift through sandy wastes, Majnun for her love
Yet none weep the heart's blood grieved by her love
Her cruelties please devotees of love
But what can be done, she'll always betray

117

On the Qualities of Master Rivalry

He had a companion ready for trial
Rivalry his name, his every word fire

He tutored that boy betwixt and between
His was the cloud bearing that pearl of dreams

He'd raised up that candle scorching the breast   1205
To light up the hall at misery's fest

He nurtured Love like a baby coal spark
So everywhere he would flame in the dark

Like men shining in the eyes of wild men
He dressed him in black again and again

He stored him like tulips for a new spring
So that his black speck would flower again

He tucked him away inside cotton fluff
So that like a wound he'd fill up with blood

He trained that boy sweet as a baby tear   1210
To make mud pies with the sand of despair

So that when that moon became fully grown
He'd stand like a tombstone facing the road

Master Rivalry Wrangles with Love

When Rivalry saw that Love was on fire
He found an opportune time to inquire

"My rosebud of hell's own garden of flame
What's happened to make you cry out in pain?

What need is there for so many cold sighs
Do you suppose that they will not suffice?

What's with you, alas, have you found a cure?   1215
Is it good health makes you weepy and dour?

If it's pain that makes you cry out and grieve
You do me a thousand wrongs, woe is me

Since pain is a thing that's borne by a man
It must be that pain's the mark of a man"

Love Answers Master Rivalry

Love scowled and shot a glance at the man
He rubbed poison in the wound with that glance

He said, "So you don't know anything yet?
You've not even heard of Beauty's name yet?

Be gone! nothing I can say is for you   1220
Be silent! this isn't what you're used to

Make haste to rush to the rescue of friends
Turn back, peace and patience are at an end

I'll fill this age with my sighs, go away!
Whatever will be, will be anyway

Where were you when I was free and at ease?
Is it just now that you've found time to speak?

I'm not here for this, come on now, don't stay
You think you'll convince me talking this way?"

Master Rivalry Answers Love

Said Rivalry, "This is friendship, my man   1225
My aim is to ease your pain, if I can

I meant no reproach to you, God forfend
Don't injure your old and trusty good friend

But sighing and grief provide no recourse
This ocean of blood will never reach shore

Renounce all this meaningless hue and cry
Don't echo on like a mountain's reply

Don't give up the ghost because of one blow
Stop crying, it's shameful, shameful, stop now!

Or did you think this was easy to do?   1230
That heartache's army would be just one troop?"

Love Answers Rivalry

Love looked at him, saying, "What is it now?
O Lord, what disaster have we met now?

Does Rivalry no more understand speech?
Or can it be stuttering now afflicts me?

Must it be that every sigh portend pain?
Is to cry invariably to complain?

Excuse me, my brave companion, excuse
It's Love's job to sigh, it's his duty to"

Rivalry Answers

Said Rivalry, "Sighs are fine, it is true   1235
But they're out of place here and have no use

There's no other side to this desert waste
And Beauty will not find this to her taste"

Love Answers

Love said to him, "You have not understood
You lack knowledge of the evil and good

If Beauty did not approve of my plea
The universe would at once cease to be

You think that my sighs are only hot air?
You think that my cries bring no force to bear?

They're all tales to lull my darling to sleep   1240
They're choruses that she sings at her feast

For Leyla it's all absurd in the end
The despair of Kays and Nawfal's amends"

Rivalry Digs Up Another Pretext

Then Rivalry heaved a breast-burning sigh
And traded the day for winter's dark night

"May God grant a thousand blessings," said he
"It seems Love knew all, and has informed me

But there must be passion in your pursuit
You need to advance your beloved's suit

Tomorrow approach the tribe, don't delay   1245
You are a shah's falcon, go seize your prey

Put weeping aside and take action now
You won't win your love by furrowing your brow

I'll be your companion, ride by your side
I'm friend of the cave in mountains of trial

With this one condition, be my support
And crush Mistress Modesty with your force

Or leave the affair to me if you will
I'll make Modesty submit to my will

This is good advice, hear well what I say   1250
For Rivalry wants no one in his way

It's Modesty's fault that Dazzle could part
The paths of two lovers sharing one heart

You too are quite well informed of it all
I don't know what fancy has you in thrall

As long as the clam's shell has not been cleaved
The pearl of desire will not be achieved"

Love Is Disgusted

"Be silent!" said Love, and bitterly cried
"For once will you not hear Poetry's side?

Does one shoot cruel arrows at his true love?   1255
That's not something you should even think of

If there's any manly spirit in you
Companion me, render me service due

Don't fear for your head or give life a thought
Consider my bargain and take a loss

Does one tell a madman how to walk right?
This raw proposition is the most ripe

Will sword unsheathed bring beloved nearer
Can everything shiny be a mirror?

Come on with me if you will lend a hand   1260
Or tell me if you have a better plan

You bring me conditions, promises made
You sing lullabies just like a nursemaid

If such-and-such happens we should do that
Or so-and-so if things turn out like that

You slip in debates from *medrese* school
And I'm to hear the entire golden rule"

Rivalry Binds Himself to Love's Service

"Here now is my vow, friend," Rivalry said
"I'll share your mind should it cost me my head

I will never open my mouth again   1265
The parrot of secrecy stays within

And if ever-changing fate should allow
I'll give my head for one hair of your brow

Don't think that I sought the easy way out
I wanted to test your ardor's redoubt

I'd not shirk my duty, weary in dread
Don't take offense at whatever I've said"

When Rivalry *jumped the sword* to join in
Love cocked an eyebrow in signal to him

"Come on with me then, let's be on our way   1270
What's done is done, no excuses today"

Love marked with a Fatiha this intent
His training in union had now commenced

Love Goes to the Tribe to Ask for Beauty's Hand

His Highness swift Love and Rivalry now
Were fixed on their goal and passionate vow

By law then Professor Madness announced
That Beauty could be won only by joust

He purposed that Love, gnawed by grief inside,
Should be informed how things were with the tribe

Each one of them sought a way to have her   1275
Each fancied himself in love with the girl

The rule of the difficult trial is known
A world full of rivals, Love all alone

The tribe came and gathered all in one place
Love stepped forward there and argued his case

"I now to the jewel of Beauty lay claim
I'll be victor in contest of this claim

If she is a pearl, then I am her shell
Two lovers succeed one another well

If Beauty's a glorious sun, shining bright,   1280
Then I am the firmament to that light

If combat for claim to her is the plan
Here are my sword and my spear, here my pen

For every foe ruined by my sword's scourge
It's I who've composed his funeral dirge"

The Tribe Ridicules Love

The lords of the Sons of Love looked away
And glanced at each other as if to say

This heart-lost boy's started to rave and rant
What is reason's cure to Majnun but cant?

Each and every one scoffed him to the skies   1285
They made the poor boy the foil of their gibes

"Don't sharpen your sword, my man," began one
"Cut down on your opium and be done"

Another, "Delusions are wondrous strange
It seems there will be no cure for this pain"

Another said, "Don't spend time writing verse
It leads to hallucinations far worse"

Another: "My Shah, your throne has been blessed
Live long! May your fortune also be blessed"

Another: "My, my, he's touched in the brain   1290
It must be his object to entertain"

Another: "That's how a high fever is
If he's not bled soon he'll go on like this"

"He's got a sword there," another complained
"But Majnun is better off when he's chained"

Another said, "Well, of course he's upset
That venture, you know, he's deeply in debt"

Doors opened for every subject to vent
Those babblers went on to their hearts' content

Some long-winded talkers picked up the thread   1295
The lecture of errors was again read

"Dear friends, if I may dare to be so bold
This rose water's quite good for a head cold"

"One time I was on my way to the bath
I saw so-and-so, and while I've said that ... "

"You mentioned the bath, it made me recall
A matter of great import above all

First, please be so kind to let me relate
How once in my service to a great sheikh ..."

127

If all that they said were told in detail   1300
Our treatise would not suffice for the tale

Those little men, with their underhand ways
Embarked on a thousand gaffes and mistakes

The *story of many branches* was aired
The causes of madness all were heard there

And so Love and Rivalry in suspense
Stood there while all had fun at their expense

Our quick hero, speechless in his distress,
Showed Beauty the deep wound torn in his breast

And this was the answer Beauty conveyed   1305
"Hear carefully everything the tribe says

Whatever decision they shall declare
That is my decision; do not despair"

Love Humbles Himself

That man of amazement was now unmanned
A slave to his mortal foes' cruel command

He asked, "What's the reason for this abuse
This fabrication the tribe's introduced?

For what reason am I made laughingstock
My words misinterpreted by foul talk?

Why do you not offer counsel to me? 1310
Is it something else but reason I speak?

If only a madman seeks Beauty now
This whole universe must be a madhouse

Explain why you find grounds for my arrest
If I have done wrong, produce evidence"

The Tribe Decides the Bride-Price Is
Endurance of Trial, according to Custom

Then all together the lords of the tribe
Explained to him what it was they desired

"O wise man who comes to seek Beauty here
If good counsel be the pearl in your ear

Consider we all know each other well 1315
We're all prone to passion and raising hell

Who is there has gained his love with one speech?
Does one flower bring springtime within reach?

Could ever there be reward without toil?
So many gain nothing even with toil

To bring on our laughter what better cause
You all of a sudden claim Beauty yours

Was ever beloved won with a word?
Indulge us and don't repeat the absurd

Don't reckon our challenge trickery and lies   1320
Ask Kays what he has to say of our tribe

Nor trial nor travail, but beloved's tryst
Is there anyone who can deserve this?

That road's not been traveled by any man
It's never been heard of by any man

As everyone knows, the crown's for the head
To wear the crown on this path, give your head"

Love Accepts the Trials

Love understood how this story would end
And no longer tried with words to contend

"Command!" he said, "Let my service commence   1325
For me trial and torment from here on hence"

The lords of the tribe then gave their advice
"You will pay a very generous bride-price

For marriage with Beauty has to be dear
First you need to bring the alchemy here

Go to the Land of the Heart straightaway
Strive with soul and body in the Heart's Way

It's said that the alchemy is found there
The path is beset with trial and despair

A snake thousand-headed with painted tail   1330
An ocean of fire where waxen ships sail

The Ruin of Heartache, thousand years' ride
The Palace of Mourning on the far side

The infamous witch who guards that highway
Has serpents for hair—that's no lie, they say

A desolate steppe with fairies and fiends
Lions and panthers, bloodthirsty beasts

Hideous genies of a thousand kinds
And dragons concealed in wizard's disguise

The voices of ghouls on black nights resound   1335
Way out in the steppe with thundering howls

Black magic makes fire rain down in the wild
And painted snakes too rain once in a while

If you with God's help reach that citadel
And drink of the water at the Heart's well

And harvest the alchemy as agreed
Return and united with Beauty be"

Love's Journey to the Land of the Heart

Love's heart was light when these tidings were told
He burst through his robe with joy thousandfold

He asked at once for the Land of Heart's way   1340
He took the road to the Heart straightaway

And Rivalry shared each thought in his head
The two friends resolving to reach the friend

That man of the road now to the road fell
And with his first step fell into a well

But what sort of well was this maelstrom pit
Like time without end, no beyond to it

"Hey warrior," Rivalry shouted out
"Ask Karun about that alchemy now"

This well was a pit of darkness supreme   1345
It stood guard at buried treasures of grief

Nor darkness-land nor the way to not-there
A pit whose insides were all cries and prayers

It signified exile's drear winter's night
A sea without shore of cruelty's fright

If Hizir immortal strayed and plunged down
His life would come up short half the way down

132

The sun with its lasso of months and years
Had no chance to ever reach bottom here

The *moon of Nahsheb* fell into that well   1350
We could fairly name it then Nahsheb's well

But don't you be grieved to ponder his fall
For Joseph's ascent began with a fall

As if from his chin there sprang curly hair
Harut met the *moon of Canaan* in there

In sum then that world-adorning sun fell
And came to nest upside-down in the well

He'd aimed for the peak of heaven at first
But his way apparently led to dirt

As many a year and month and day passed   1355
He came to rest at the bottom at last

And as it turned out that well of torment
Was lair where a demon rested content

A demon with many regiments strong
A quarry of blackness each single one

A night of exile all dread-faced and coarse
A bloodthirsty stinking elephant's corpse

Those two poor unfortunates were then seized
Roped with lassos, dragged away by the feet

They brought them before the beast in his cups　　1360
And said, "Here's today's catch, though it's not much"

That demon opaque demanded of Love
Like Saturn now face-to-face with the sun

"Say, where did you mean to go when you fell
With such ill-digested thought in this well?

I've heard it's for Beauty you grieve and pine
You seek gold and you're a slave to the mine

But what kind of cockeyed plan have you made?
This isn't wit but a world full of pain

Where are you and where is that brilliant sun?　　1365
Where is the sea, where the mirage of one?

Your flesh is for us a fortunate find
Your eyesight and vision both have gone blind

Who's been to the land of alchemy, hah!
Who's found the *Anka* or seen the *Huma*?

You didn't ask, didn't think, off you went
And fell in a well upon your first step

Good God, how exceeding dumb can one be
In ignorance there's no further degree

I pity your youth, it is quite a shame　　1370
But your misconception is wondrous strange!"

Love Is Enraged

Love boiled with the fire of rancor unleashed
And said, "There's no need for this lukewarm speech

It's murder you want, is that not your plan?
Injustice and justice yours to command

As if with these words my beloved's thought
Could be in my heart by one dust mote lost

You'll not frighten me, so don't waste your breath
For me union is my hour of death

It's not I alone who keep her in mind   1375
The weeds will keep moaning if I should die

The reeds in this well grow higher and higher
To sing to lovers of pain of exile

This passion will not take leave of my brain
This smoke rising from my hearth will remain

It's heartache's torch and can never go out
I'll give my life, but I'll never turn round"

The Demon Throws Them into Prison

That ill-fated demon, cursed and damned
Had them thrown in prison by his command

So that their fat and their flesh might increase   1380
And later be victual for that fiend's feast

So there Rivalry and Love did both stay
As prisoners of pain for many a day

They gave one another comfort and cheer
And strengthened each other to persevere

Poetry Comes to the Rescue

One fine morn sage Poetry rescued them
He stood at the well's mouth calling to them

"Imprisoned there in the well, O brave youths
Dear friends in the time of trial and abuse

Set out toward salvation, do not delay   1385
The way's full of danger, do not delay

No salvation can be found down in there
No refuge for those who fall down in there

Except for a rope hid deep in the pit
The jinn there do not have knowledge of it

A spell was inscribed thereon by a sage
With many a sacred safeguarding name

Whoever will take that rope and hold firm
Is saved by the *name supreme* from all harm

The jinn cannot hurt him, he will go free   1390
Escaping to find salvation and peace

I've said all of this by means of a spell
The jinn cannot hear and you must not tell"

Love and Rivalry Find Salvation

Those two tightrope walkers cleaved to his words
And with divine aid became the victors

When sky-seizing Love then opened his eyes
He saw that it had been Poetry wise

He knew this was from the beloved's clime
He knew this dawn broke upon that springtime

With longing and grief he heaved a deep sigh   1395
"By God, speak to me of Beauty," he cried

"Of what does she dream? Does she speak of me?
Does she not at times recall feeble me?

Is she not informed of how we despair?
Does she not at all inquire how we fare?

Does she never call her old friends to mind?
Is she at all pleased by how we are tried?

It's with that desire I fell in the well
That I might be near to her in the well

But later I heard this was a mistake   1400
The zenith of heaven is the moon's place

And now I am shamed to fail in my quest
I've plunged in the earth but I've found no rest

It would have been fit had I expired there
You came to my rescue like Hizir there

But now speak to me of her, give me news
That's over, now from my love bring me news"

But Poetry paid no mind to these moans
Transformed as a bird he took swift wing home

"Hey brother," called Rivalry, "we must go   1405
The road is the place for men of the road"

And spreading their wings, two *Humas* on high,
They swooped down the road like owls of exile

They wielded the span of sight as a rod
Like men of the eyes of trial and took off

They'd fallen, now heartache increased their load
The Ruin of Heartache fell cross their road

That place had been mentioned on the first day
A pit of despair each step of the way

Night and the Violence of Winter

They lost the path in a land black and wild   1410
The long night of winter, unforeseen trial

In God we take refuge from such a clime
The jinn played at polo there all the time

Despair and terror were welded as one
At times snow, at times black darkness rained down

There snow was the consort of darkest night
Combined in one form were darkness and light

Congealed in the cold the light of the moon
Dripped down like quicksilver instead of dew

The winter night was a frozen white deer   1415
Musk mixed in with camphor filled the steppe here

It seemed that dark night by snow intertwined
Were like the eye's black orb therein confined

The heavens' azure skies cracked, frozen hard
And fell down to earth in fragment and shard

Look here how black-deeded fortune afar
Is holding a mirror to Zanzibar

The cold formed with snow the mouth of a stream
The black man of night grinned showing his teeth

The stars lost in darkness of winter's gloom   1420
The thousand-pinned horseshoe of the bright moon

The roads and the squares were like Leo's sign
Wherever you looked, a fluffy white lion

The tongue of flame froze and stuttering took hold
The cry of flame chattered, trembling with cold

The sparks of rebellion froze in the ice
Fire glowed frozen tight inside pearls of ice

The glass windows in the bathhouse were cracked
It seemed by a diamond dome to be capped

The cold mountain torrents took off in flight   1425
And rained down again but this time as ice

The border of silver took stock and fled
To stay in Sütlüce round a flower bed

There brother fought brother and spilled his blood
Their fingers and fists were bright coral red

A black scribbling wrapped the terrified globe
The mountains whirled in step with the cyclone

Not one rebel bird was left in the sky
Though now and again fire's color would fly

The ruby-like froth of bubbling red wine   1430
Had no need to fear the heat of the fire

From inside of fire pure spring water broke
Encircling the cyclone all round with smoke

The folk who went out to fish in the cold
Had lines baited end to end with hot coals

The sky's green dome would have faded to dust
If pillars of ice had not held it up

December's sultan decked out the whole town
From lips of the roofs silver flutes hung down

Tongues froze as they spoke into icy chips   1435
A grumbling sound rose from the roofs' lips

The sun's fire temple would have blown away
If dawn hadn't hammered down ice tent stays

Mistaking the oceans for grassy fields
The antelopes grazed on fish for their meals

If dogs' mouths had foamed white froth to the ground
The hares would have thought their lost fathers found

The fairies who feared they might slip and fall
Would not come near pools or pond banks at all

If spring's February heat had not swooned   1440
It would not have dropped down to earth till June

Men's natures steamed manifest through their lips
No less than ice hanging from the roofs' lips

141

When people with trembling breath would converse
They spoke diamond chains of raving mad words

The glittering candles under fine shades
Shone like coral branches 'neath ocean waves

The dove in its cage was too stunned to cry
To see *heaven's vulture* cooped in the sky

So sparrows would not peck grains of chagrin   1445
There spark feed was scattered round by children

The cold was so harsh the hands of Mars froze
His dagger clattered down from heaven's dome

The zodiac's Leo rolled up in snow
For teeth, when he grinned, the Pleiades glowed

To light up the night instead of a star
The day of victory blazed from afar

Their tears freezing on their eyes as they wept
Men wearing ice eyeglasses searched for death

In order to find again the heart's flame   1450
Sworn foes the most intimate friends became

The deer ran to graze gunpowder for feed
The partridges pecked at gun primer reed

Wine drinking and self-denial, one at last
Fire water the same as fire-blown glass

And strangest of all, the road of thought froze
Fine genius was paralyzed in the poets

The wordsmiths were silent, every last one
The wine vats of meaning stayed flat and calm

O Galip, they'll never be match for me   1455
The fire of thought cannot catch up with me

Conclusion

In that fear and danger Love the aware
Was lost in a thousand kinds of sad terror

This plain was no city, that he knew well
But it must be alchemy or a spell

The means of destruction were manifold
With thunder and lightning and freezing cold

A black sea of gloom crashed wave upon wave
While troop after troop of ghoul visions raved

On one side the trial of fantasy's swarm   1460
On one side the blinding cold of the storm

He'd never seen Heartache's Ruin before
He'd always been spoiled by time and adored

He saw darkness flood the land and still spread
It plunged that poor boy in horror and dread

143

He roamed around wildly, raced to and fro
He searched like a whirlwind vain high and low

No path was there to be found on that plain
No exit there that he could ascertain

He suddenly saw it, taken aback   1465
A terrible fire heaped up in a stack

A sign of the boiling pitch of hellfire
With tongue upon tongue of roaring red fire

The smoke of its flames reached up to the skies
This was sorcery but shown in flame's guise

The Witch

An old hag made her abode in that place
A frightful witch with a dread demon's face

Like Satan himself she dwelled in hellfire
Surrounded by boiling pitch, steam and tar

Her head could with Montenegro compete   1470
Old infidel tombstones for mouth and teeth

She had Modaburnu plain for a nose
All hyena dens and deep lizard holes

Her lower lip sagged as low as her knees
She stank like a dying elephant's wheeze

Her two eyes like tortoises colored drab
Her eyelashes like the feet of a crab

For eyebrows she had two black centipedes
Her hair was like vipers snarling in heaps

Her breasts were like two pigs strung on a nail   1475
She'd hung upside down to offer for sale

Her two ears were furrows dug up by moles
The dens of hedgehogs or filthy rat holes

There streamed from her mouth disgusting foul fluids
That smelled as bad and as putrid as sewers

With worms, mice and scorpions in her nose
Her mouth full of snakes and lizards and moles

Whenever she spoke, her tongue spat out fire
As if the cruel monster of that hellfire

She kept tools of witchcraft close at her side   1480
A thousand old pots and oils of all kinds

Each time that she cast an oil in the brew
Fancies by the thousand came into view

She'd ride like the wind on top of a cloud
She'd even make fire itself cry out loud

She bore progeny from under her arm
Fed on blood from babies she had gulped down

And then she would eat the children she bore
That evil abomination, once more

The Witch Propositions Love

She chanted a spell and beckoned Love forth   1485
Displaying herself in finery adorned

Bright radiant silks, a thousand brocades
Pearls, rubies and diamonds with gold inlay

Those shimmering robes were instantly donned
She called out to Love, "Come and take me, son

Have mercy, dear, marry this pining maid
My heart's chosen you, it must be obeyed

Of all the whole world I'll make you sultan
For your humble slave it's easily done

If this business should arouse your distaste   1490
I'll cast such a spell I'll lay you to waste"

Love listened and understood what he heard
At first he wept, then he found it absurd

He raised up his head to face heaven then
That knows all the secrets of jinn and men

And making the sky's disk shield for his sigh
He called lovely sun-faced Beauty to mind

"O Beauty, O sun who lights up the dark
O you who imprison Love in a spark

Is this what I'd hoped of you, O my moon?   1495
A foul witch after me, lusting and lewd?

I powerless, trapped in thrall of exile
You living in ease and pleasure meanwhile?

While I'm lost in snow and darkness hemmed in
Shall these heavens whirl by grace of your whim?

Can this be the way that friends show their love?
Ah, be fair with me, sweet moon up above!

She who keeps her lover slaved on hot coals
Won't feel Kevser's water pass down her throat"

Now heaven, now she he loved, and now fate   1500
Kept his searing tears on sale like hot cakes

Love Is Crucified by the Witch

The witch saw him struggling in this unease
And increased her enmity by degrees

She strung him up on a cross with a word
And made him a target for spit and sword

With Rivalry Love hung facing that pyre
So that they'd take admonition from fire

By hanging the shah, that cruel sorceress
Outdid Nimrod himself in Nimrod-ness

He'd already seen the bottomless pit   1505
This time round the *catapult* was deemed fit

That flower of dew like mosque candlelight
Burned by dint of hanging all the more bright

The witch did like Love and so by all this
She meant just to scare him out of his wits

Although his throat seized with terror and hurt
His innocent soul was not at all hurt

That jasmine-skinned boy hung there mild and meek
Like parson in pulpit week after week

So various were his thousandfold wails   1510
Those passing by thought they heard nightingales

Sometimes he assailed the skies' tyranny
And sometimes he sighed and cried to Beauty

When luck was the subject of his approach
He sharpened the arrow of his reproach

"O fortune, how can you so betray me?
Have you no affection at all for me?

Let's take the beloved, she should be false
It suits her and is her way, after all

The lover must suffer heartbreak and trial   1515
While she must be faithless, she must beguile

But you at least shouldn't play the coquette
Come, don't you too try to be fashion's pet"

But neither this nor that bore any weight
He saw it was all the working of fate

As consciousness flooded back to his mind
He called the thought of God's mercy to mind

"Creator of man and jinn, have mercy!
I am powerless, oh please have mercy!

If union with her is not fate's to give   1520
Reclaim my life, let that winsome maid live"

Besieged by a thousand thoughts, mortified
He called on the one he worshipped and cried

At that moment Poetry was there seen
He came like God's word *"Be!"* from the unseen

That instant the night of darkness dispersed
Pure joy took the place of horror and hurt

Truth manifest, gone illusions that seemed
The sorcery turned to dust like false dreams

When riotous Love saw that sage he wept   1525
He tore and he rent asunder his breast

Recalling then Beauty he sighed and moaned
This poetry sweet and pure he composed

Lyric

Well met, messenger of the beloved
Glad tidings bestow from the beloved
Slay me at the feast of the beloved
Is my hope in vain of the beloved?
Does she not send any greeting for me?

O Hizir, the guide for those who fall, speak
This mystery now reveal to me, speak   1530
You be my interpreter, for me speak
Keep nothing back, tell all one by one, speak
Will there be no sum to grief's registry?

My God, what is this intolerable suspense
This wind never stops, it never relents
Forever these sorrows, pains and laments
If I only knew what was this pretense
Has she no desire for union with me?

Like Mansur I climbed the scaffold so tall
My cry is the Judgment's trumpet prayer call   1535
Grief makes my throat groan the bass flute's low call
The soldiers of trial now hold me in thrall
Has that padishah no message for me?

The beggars have all they once sought of fate
While friends till tomorrow are told to wait
Don't those oaths, those pledges, still stand in place?
Will she not accept the prayers I have made?
Is her heart's design all inconstancy?

Astonished by grief, I have no words left
Like Galip, I've not an ounce of strength left   1540
The plea that I sent has not been addressed
At this moment there is just one chance left
Does justice have no name in that country?

Poetry Announces the Good News

Then Poetry raised the gate of address
Delivering forth his answer like this

"Did you think your friend had no news of you?
Or did you suppose she'd forsaken you?

She's shah of the Land of Beauty and Grace
It's she who saves those who fall in disgrace

Don't think her beloved, she is the lover   1545
Heed this word of truth more than any other

The power behold of Beauty peerless
See what has become of that sorceress

With open eyes take a careful look now
From this take instruction, where's the witch now?"

Then Love who adorns the world looked to see
He glanced over where the witch had to be

But what did he see? She was a strange mess
All stuffed in a sack, a dog's old carcass

No jewels, no trinkets, no fine outfits   1550
The corpse of a pig, an infidel stiff

Struck down by a sword, she'd been sliced in two
Once evil in deed, now evil-starred too

Nor fire nor darkness at her command
No blizzard, no cross, no terror to withstand

Then Poetry gave a shape to that dream
And thus he explained what had before seemed

"Because you forgot to say Beauty's name
The witch could confound and put you to shame

Beauty's name is talisman to that spell   1555
Her name abrogates the power of that spell

You called upon her in your hour of need
What happened, happened then, she intervened

Peerless Beauty heard and answered your call
And sent you in gift this bejeweled sword

The Sword of Ah!

But what a sword! Diamond from head to toe
The firebolt of Satan, scourge to the foe

One leaf from the *double blade* of Ali
One verse from the epic wars of Ali

In combat the mirror of divine aid   1560
The guide Hizir of the padishah's way

The envy of sabers of eye and brow
It forced satirists to silently bow

A river of blood, a fiery flume
A snake multicolored, poison of doom

A crescent moon served it for brilliant sheath
End to end in substance the Pleiades

One pulse of the spring of youth eternal
Diamond, but its whetstone was red coral

A sword such as this was sea without shore   1565
Where instead of water pure spirit flowed

The mighty claws of the glittering sun
Had drawn it forth from the breast of the moon

It glanced like a pretty girl's teasing eyes
And jeered at the tumult of fate's demise

The moon of the sky of combat most cruel
A bright swordfish spinning round trial's whirlpool

A flame-bearing branch from arbors of fire
All carved in gold work with form of pure fire

A fountain of liquid ruby thirst-quenched   1570
An emerald stream that glowed black as jet

A green parrot with a bloody mustache
A falcon who pheasant-faced sought its catch

The angel of death its signal obeyed
The beat of its wings raised up Judgment Day

The one who lays wealth down in the mine's chute
Drew it from the bird's breast of Melekut

The peace of protection seen in its might
The *chain mail of David*, its gleam of light

A bird greenest green who carries black news   1575
And under its wing the *death of red hue*

Bloodthirsty, but it was tyranny-proof
To casuistry a reply absolute

This will be a witness serving your cause
Don't look awry, this is the Sword of Ah!

Whatever obstruction may block your way
Dispatch to the Sword of Ah! straightaway

Sorrel Rose

That fairy girl also has sent for you
A heart-stealing sorrel horse rose in hue

A pheasant-like sorrel rose-colored steed   1580
A heavenly rose-bed blood-swelling sea

A liquid of ruby rolling in waves
Like Refref who takes the road Lahut way

Spring dressed up in roses from head to foot
Like ruby wine bubbling mischief afoot

Like quicksilver but with figure of flame
Alike to the sun a picture of flame

In form subtlety all kneaded like dough
Like glimpses of resurrection in flow

Tuba of the heavens, bright tree of flame   1585
A mansion in Eden, high throne of flame

She was alike to the lover's heart's blood
Hizir's spring of youth immortal, but blood

Magnificent lion, heaven's peacock
A gorgeous young bride in vermillion frock

When she gathered speed and galloped by fast
The end of the future heard from its past

When she wished, her gait left with its swift thrust
Instants indivisible in the dust

She sped by so fast her gallop was such   1590
She'd leave the motes of the air all untouched

When she set her mind to covering space
She outstripped the parts of time in a race

Rose-bodied piebald steeds envied her when
She moved like Shirin and stood like Rustem

Sometimes on one hoof arresting her gait
She made the Black Sea seem all stony slate

That flame figure mountain-firm at a halt
Was like Mars aloft in his ruby vault

Her two ears a royal falcon's aigrette   1595
A crystal decanter served as her neck

An animal but eternal youth's spring
A coral palm tree, a morning in spring

Each string of her mane a *tambur*'s gay tune
Whenever she neighed, Doomsday's trumpet blew

Her hoof like a skull cupped white devils' brains
The hairs of her tail were shining sun rays

She flowed down like water through mine and earth
She leaped up like flame upon heaven's berth

Her breast was a lion, her eyes were shy deer　　1600
She had dragon's breath and hyacinth hair

An *Anka* endowed with poetic speech
In flight she was conjured flame beyond reach

She glowed with the color of tears of blood
She struck accord with the *kanun* of love

Alike to a parrot though all in red
She silenced the pen in deep ruby red

Expansive, enthralling, charmingly sweet
The pleasure of wine that calms the wild beast

In short, fleet-winged Sorrel Rose surely will　　1605
Convey you on to the Heart's citadel

These are souvenirs from Beauty to you
But this is the Land of Heartache, strive through

She sent Rivalry too pinions and wings
And strength to companion you in all things

What padishah is she, do you not see
That Love's guide upon the true path is she?

You wonder how Beauty, that peerless flower
Has come in possession of this great power

I'm her humble slave, that's all that I am　　1610
I'm naught but dust at her feet, understand

Whenever that sovereign should command me
All these things would be as nothing to me"

His Majesty Love got up on that steed
And set out on down the road with all speed

And Rivalry spread wing and pinion wide
They called union with that shah into mind

Love's Weariness

It seemed now to Love a burdensome pain
Sometimes he would feel that all was in vain

To leave the beloved, take to the road   1615
To leave the moon and then sink down so low

He grew more discouraged each passing day
Each mile seemed to bring him farther away

Said Rivalry, "But hope is never lost
Can God's omnipresent grace be far off?

To reach the goal travelers go in reverse
It's vagabonds who discover the pearl

All know God the Truth has nor front nor back
He has no direction, cannot be tracked

Let's make haste to strive by night and by day   1620
We are sure to see that sun one fine day"

That perfect full moon each night persevered
And traveled the space of one thousand years

That radiant sun each day kept apace
The span of *nine heavens'* vasty broad space

Like Jesus he rode astride the bright sun
The journey for him was not a long one

And when to the fear of death he'd fall prey
That pitiless boy heard Rivalry say

"Death lasts not like exile long as one lives   1625
Is there aught his slave can't bear that God gives?"

On the Qualities of the Fortress of Forms

O Saki, bring out the fire of red wine
With that fire within let my spirit shine

Let uproar of weeping eyes fill my heart
Let waves of the flood crash into my hearth

Let this my breast burn, a city on fire
But let it be drowned in flames of wine's fire

We're bound by love to the church organ's strings
And chained in the wave of blood's roiling swings

There's nothing can cut asunder our gyves   1630
Except for the sword blade of waves of wine

159

Give that wine to me now with such a rage
Its froth with be bloody Mars of outrage

Let that rosy cup now lead me astray
And bring me in concord with Mansur's way

Let evil and good from thought be erased
Let life and death lock in one fond embrace

Grief's ruin was just a slaughtering field
Where is that enchanted cup now concealed?

The road's overgrown by brambles and weeds   1635
Let torrents of sparks come and sweep it clean

I range Heartache's desert from end to end
Who now is there dares with me to contend?

Let those come on here who would bar my way
Those yearning to taste the Sword of Ah!'s blade!

Love Leaves the Ruin of Heartache

His Majesty Love, the fearless and brave
Plunged full of desire upon Heartache's plain

When lightning-swift Love then struck with that sword
He ground into rubble all Heartache's ward

Each evil ghoul there who strayed cross his path   1640
He tossed to the Sword of Ah! like a scrap

To take the sky's place he made earth turn round
Instead of the Milky Way snakes shone down

He put on display the ghouls' severed heads
And paid to those soldiers wages of death

He spilt of the blood of lions oceans wide
And spattered the desert like leopard's hide

That angel-born lad with one single sword
Made paradise from hell's night of discord

The Ruin of Heartache now was short work   1645
He saw apparitions and witch's work

He passed by the hour of death just in time
The Palace of Mourning was left behind

He'd heard before he would meet the next trial
Wax ships launched upon an ocean of fire

Now all at once it was there on his road
An ocean of flame to burn up the soul

That ocean was home to many a fiend
Who lived in wax ships they brought into being

That demon race can't be injured by fire   1650
Can fire ever harm a creature of fire?

They held the ships up suspended on air
And captured so many poor fools passing there

Whoever approached to board on a ship
Those demons would execute him forthwith

Like bridal palms carried at feasts in train
Their rosy hulls glowed bright-figured in flame

Islands of catastrophe, one might say
All brimming with pain, a crimson doomsday

A likeness of Surhab Mountain each one   1655
Filled with demons, each a mountain's stepson

These wax ships all looked like coffins on view
But where they'd be buried nobody knew

Those ships and that raging fire full of doom
Were candles that had been lit by a tomb

The site of that sorcery was but fire
No harm to the shore did thereby transpire

The demons bid Love to board on a ship
They said he'd be safe and sound on a ship

But Love understood it all in a flash   1660
He tried to be patient and not be rash

However, the road was blocked, what to do?
There was to be seen no other way through

He Ponders the State of His Soul

"Omnipotent God, creator, how long?
This torment and pain and torment, how long?

What bandit can strike when all roads are yours?
If you seek desire, then that too is yours

Must all who are driven wild by desire
Mount high like Mansur upon scaffold's wire?

Don't make pain of exile target my breast   1665
Why put a man of bad faith to the test?

You've made me display one dust mote of love
And raised my head up high as the proud sun

Don't leave me here slave to sorcerers now
Slay me but don't leave me ailing here now

That death would be life eternal for me
Although it's a bane desired selfishly

The goal must be resignation of self
But you must bestow intention itself

My feet are bound on the path seeking you   1670
You must show the way, what else can I do?

Grant me an appeal that you can accept
Both teach me to pray and my prayer accept

Bestow on my heart the grace of desire
And give me the grace fit for my desire

Let subtlety couple with my request
Perfection replace my gross impudence

If I'll have the gallows, there be my mosque
If fire, then the fire shall be where I halt

If God's sea of grace rise in waves divine   1675
His servants can never be far from mind

I know this grief doesn't merit a sigh
By God, it's not worth the glance of an eye

But hope for your mercy is the object
Your kindness is what we've come to expect

You gave freely in the desert of naught
The raiment of being when it was not

This instant we are but naught, in naught still
The *boon universal* is what we will"

———————————

A prisoner of longing, he lingered there   1680
Nor thought of return nor power to forbear

His rose-bodied mount was moved to speak up
"For what reason have you come to a stop?"

Love wept, pouring out the pearls of his tears
The words that he spoke came rolling like pearls

"I've no wings like Rivalry to fly higher
What will become of me here in this fire?

I am not a falcon that I should fly
And soar many thousand miles in the sky"

But Sorrel Rose like the *Anka* took flight   1685
And glided across that fire without fright

A fire with smoke like smoke of Nimrod
And black ghouls like specters of cruel Nimrod

The whole world in fire of grief was aflame
There whirlpools were wells of hell all aflame

A hell where quicksilver flame flowers burst
It took a whirlpool to slake each coal's thirst

Rose-colored like passion's very own blood
An ocean of sparks, a high sea of blood

Each wave an encircling ocean of fire   1690
Its depths were infernal pits of hellfire

Then Rivalry said, "Don't torture yourself!
This fire is that alchemy's fire itself

Soar up like the eagle, take wing and fly
In trial's crucible prove yourself well tried

Don't think you'll go through this gate with regret
To go down in fire and end up all wet

It's fire of *mortality*, do not run
Don't go in the *horse's belly* again"

Love made the perfection of Love wax strong   1695
He rose like the sun in blood of the dawn

The sparks rose in waves up higher and higher
In flight Sorrel Rose climbed higher and higher

The ocean of fire was roiling with bane
That ravishing roan appeared like a flame

His cold sigh like Abraham's *"Fire, be cold ..."*
Rose over those flames like fine wafting smoke

And Rivalry spread his wings by his side
He flew like a moth with face of a lion

That radiant sun left in smoke adrift   1700
Was mischief caused by a lunar eclipse

With each moment he dispatched a ghoul's soul
Straight off to hell with one blow of his sword

Beneath him his *salamander*-like horse
Beside him brave Rivalry keeping close

In sum, he sped down that fiery road
As cool as the breeze that moves with the dawn

He came to a shoreline on the far side
Like spring in the garden of paradise

Its nightingales were bright parrots that spoke   1705
Its parakeets knew both anguish and hope

The greenery flowed in waves like a sea
Each sapling in bloom like the Tuba tree

The flood of its grass an emerald sea
An emerald universe, earth, sky, green

In every direction flowers bloomed for miles
Like moon-faced girls full of laughter and smiles

A joyous spring bursting from every bud
Each dewdrop a moisture-laden bright cloud

That luminous garden was like the sky   1710
Each sunflower had a sun for an eye

Carnations and narcissus everywhere
The humblest weed was a hyacinth there

The atmosphere had such subtle perfume
The nightingales smelled like roses in bloom

Dust motes blooming open in the sunlight
Were like timepiece flowers they were so bright

The burrs and the thorns that grew in the grass
Would make even fortune's wheel smile and laugh

When Love looked upon those gardens and   1715
    groves
He opened his wound again with a groan

Recalling the Pleasure Place of his home
This poetry fresh as spring he composed

Lyric

How sweet was that time when my heart was glad
When happiness was my soul's native land
I think now of those desires I once had
O fortune, for God's sake, let justice stand!
Back then I was the adornment of time

This soul of mine had a garden for home
Where paradise was inside every rose   1720
Misfortune arrived and took all I owned
My heart still recalls that joy of my home
The wine of regard's enchantment was mine

Of fortune I'd not the slightest request
All pleasure that life can give, I possessed
Close by my side strolled my graceful cypress
The secret within me was concealed yet
I drew even fresh Spring's envious eye

I've fallen now to be patient in grief
I've fallen in spring a nightingale's plea   1725
Through fire I fell to the shore of the sea
I fell like a glass and cracked piece by piece
I drank the wine of my beloved's sigh

Alas, ah, those times are now past and gone
The bitterly weeping rose now is gone
The scaffold is here and my love is gone
My soul thirsts and yet wine sickness is gone
Together my love and I would drink wine

My lover and I took pleasure and rest
I rose like a whirlpool to passion's crest   1730
I dressed the wine feast in a flame-red vest
I shamed the nightingales into silence
Like Galip I'd gained all that I desire

Poetry, in the Form of a Parrot, Gives Warning

Reciting this dewy fresh poem aloud
That moon of a sudden heard a strange sound

A parrot bright green with crimson red beak
Called out from its perch these words to repeat

"That bloodthirsty child of China's great shah
Will come to this grove like rose-scattering dawn

Oh shame, what a pity, valiant youth!—yet   1735
You will fall in love with that cruel coquette

Without doubt you'll reach the Fortress of Form
There she will subject you to grievous harm"

Love looked up as pride expanded his chest
The secret within him now manifest

He cried "Alas!" and recalled Beauty's name
"Should I prove to love another? Oh shame!"

That green parrot having this much disclosed
Joined Hizir on his invisible road

And full then of passion, what did Love see?   1740
There came to that grove a band of houris

A moon with a train of ravishing girls
A luminous sun amidst whirling stars

An army of angels all of them pure
Like intellect's penetrating soldiers

That moon was the royal shah of the group
Padishah was she of that fairy troop

The gaze of a houri viewing the soul
The likeness perfect of Beauty behold

The rose of her cheek in sweet heaven dwelt   1745
The sword of her glance swift severance dealt

Her brows opened *mercy's book* with a prayer
Her lips symbolized the stream of Kevser

The glittering crystal cups of her cheeks
Strew drops of red wine upon the sun's cheeks

An icon with jasmine-silvery skin
But silent she was as form's ever been

Gestures were the only discourse she used
That moon had no mouth, what else could she do?

That infidel girl could not pronounce words   1750
Her dragoman smile translated for her

That sun who adorns the world was in brief
With ravishing Beauty all of a piece

They differed in one respect, Beauty spoke
While this was a jasmine-fragrant, dumb rose

With thousandfold feints she let her veil fall
Love froze like a picture hung on a wall

He wondered, "Is this moon Beauty?" perplexed
"Who buried the cache of fire in my breast?

Or is she the fairy guarding this land   1755
And this fairy troop here at her command?"

While Love kept repeating this train of thought
His efforts to find a thread came to naught

A throne was brought forth all studded with jewels
Conveyed by that band of light-visaged girls

They seated that moon-like girl on the throne
Or sun in a pool of light mirrored shone

She cast an attentive glance around her
And ordered that Love be called unto her

They brought him into her presence at once   1760
There light was submerged in light all at once

The feast resurrected there on that night
Bestowed new life with thousandfold delight

She showed to Love all the signs of respect
As he sat beside her as honored guest

The Feast of Pleasure

Immediately the red wine was brought
That moon blended spirit into the draught

The salver of gold was a brilliant sun
The chalices shone like stars thereupon

That shah clasped within her bower's embrace   1765
Held moon-like Love close within her embrace

In wave upon wave, the wine and the cup
Served round upon round to moon and nimbus

The fiery wine crested riotously
Vessels could have swum there as on a sea

The wine was vermillion as bloody dusk
It jeered at the moon in rosy red cups

Though fluid, its disposition was jewel
Ruby ink for disquisition at school

An essence flame-born, with flavor to please   1770
Each sip spawned a thousand sincerities

A wine that was pressed from pure peacock's blood
A spectrum of myriad pleasures when drunk

The musicians roused and started to play
The singer's entranced voice shivered like flame

A goblet of light in fair *saki*'s hand
Gave rosebuds as if from a crystal branch

The *saki* none but that fairy herself
A houri whose wine was fire itself

The tray was a pool where cups of pure wine   1775
Bobbed at the edge, golden, narcissus-fine

The cups and carafe embraced in a whirl
No drunk sees the difference twixt dust and pearl

That day in the market there was no lull
All vessels left empty came right back full

173

Surveying the scene, the pitcher praised God
Its head never rose from a prostrate nod

Moon merged in the moonbeam, moonbeam in moon
Wine in the carafe, carafe in wine swooned

The sea of fire strolled out on promenade   1780
To view wine boil up like a tidal wave

Like garnet the purple grape of the draught
Like diamond the crystal light of the cup

When angered the *saki* got in a mood
The wine was stripped like *raki* of all hue

Its color flew and the wine was so pale
It sang for the cup like a nightingale

Shame welled up in Love's pure breast jasmine-fine
And *raki* blushed deep as purple-red wine

In one single breath, that fairy-born doll   1785
Made milk in a glass the blood of Ferhad

The hand of her glance held glittering glass
As firm as the soul in Azrail's grasp

Each glance made him drink a thousand cups down
While she eyed the Sword of Ah! up and down

She kept Love distracted with that delight
He said to himself, "That sword's within sight"

174

What Happened to Love

She took his sword in that rose-colored dawn
Left heartbroken Love to weep and was gone

When riotous Love looked round at the scene   1790
Nor houri nor fairy was to be seen

No moon and no train of glittering stars
No throne covered all with gems and no shah

His heart began twisting in coils of dread
He suffered a thousand kinds of torment

What seemed union was but severance, alas!
There's no peace for lovers, no peace, alas!

The end brought all the beginning had borne
The twilight of evening fell on night's morn

Because Love thought she was the Beauty he   1795
        wooed
He trusted that coquette's face and was fooled

A treacherous road, the Sword of Ah! gone
That infamous image left him alone

Without strength to move on or stay and fight
Love and Rivalry were faced with their plight

The more he surveyed that garden of pain
The deeper the wound of exile became

Astonished and dumbfound at that fair form
Believing her Beauty, he wept and mourned

Poetry, in the Form of a Pheasant, Gives Warning

He then heard a pheasant raise rebellion   1800
And this was the fiery song the bird sung

"That girl is the daughter of China's shah
She's not Beauty, she's the image of gall

Her name is Mind Robber and that princess
Is man-killer with a fairy countenance

Tomorrow if that moon comes to this grove
She'll take you, ah! to the Fortress of Forms"

Love tried to collect his wits, but in vain
He kept burning like a candle in flame

That rose blooming bright in unity's tower   1805
Was left to haunt exile's ruin like an owl

In time the princess like flowering jasmine
Returned to nest in that garden again

She cast cautious glances round near and far
And gazed upon Love *as things truly are*

He drank of that quintessentially pure wine
The ocean of passion swelled and rose high

She made her intention known with a sign
And Love was at once drawn straight to her side

He took the way to the Fortress of Forms   1810
That shah without peer thus fell to the road

While mounting his noble horse Sorrel Rose
That ravishing boy made ready to go

And heard Rivalry cry, "No, master, no!
You'll wander astray with her, do not go

You heard what that pheasant-like parrot said
I'll not by my silence give you license"

"But brother," replied Love, "didn't you see?
That shah's as like Beauty as she could be

She is in her face so like to the friend   1815
It would be fit if I died by her hand

Is not the goal to accept divine will?
Are you not content to bear with me still?"

And so steadfast Rivalry kept his troth
He followed that boy, although he be lost

When Rivalry, Love and that fair princess
Arrived all together at the fortress

What did they see? A bizarre citadel
Its walls hung with paintings unparalleled

When they entered in through one of its gates   1820
It instantly closed and faded away

That ravishing lady, too, disappeared
Imprisoning Love and Rivalry there

On the Qualities of the Fortress of Forms

A fortress alike to shrine Sumenat
Each one of its black stones the goddess Lat

The market was painted like a church nave
A city of marvels without a gate

The homeland of Joseph each lane and route
Each wall hung with portraits of gorgeous youths

Adorned like the sphere of the zodiac   1825
Designed like Zuleyha's room to entrap

Carved images pictured Mount Bisutun
Shirins represented by tulip moons

Each one of its domes handmade by Ferhad
But each brick a tomb to bury Ferhad

Made all by imagination's sweet charm
Each form tribute from the city of form

Carved marbles with colorless filigree
Walls hung with fine paintings done by Mani

Each minaret was a *fantasy shade*   1830
A novelty gift designed for the age

The figures engraved there were delicate
Like imagery from the poems of Shavkat

The forms there from matter were disengaged
Presenting themselves uniquely half faced

The one who had painted all those portraits
Was none but that jeering Chinese princess

Fantastic like lovers' most cherished dreams
A trick never in this world to be seen

That cruel tease had to these pictures applied   1835
Paintbrushes of lashes from fairies' eyes

Their colors brought even Mani to shame
Vermillion concocted from Behzad's brain

That sun of the dawn of China, in short,
Was she who had decorated that fort

Love scrutinized each and every profile
For Beauty he heaved a sigh of exile

Then Rivalry cried, "Go, mount Sorrel Rose!
"Don't stay in this fortress, take to the road!"

When Love without peer astride Sorrel Rose   1840
Raised up heavenward the dust of the road

He started mysteriously to cross time
Each instant he went a thousand months' ride

But when the sun had reached far as the west
He'd not even gone the space of two steps

Still locked up inside the Fortress of Forms
He pondered his state, weeping and forlorn

Now everything that had happened before
Recurred again in this fortress once more

He fell in a well as he had done then   1845
The demon's ghoul army seized him again

He crossed through the freezing snow-covered steppe
He saw that ill-omened cruel fate of death

He struggled against the sorceress vile
And once more he faced that ocean of fire

Beset by so many soul-wrenching fears
He sighed and he wailed and cried out for years

In thousandfold fright Love made his way now
For he didn't have the Sword of Ah! now

When all of a sudden spirit's path cleared   1850
And Love the unique now saw there revealed

He'd come to the same place where he'd begun
Those forms and that fort locked by talisman

He cried and petitioned God the adored
He told the tale of the suffering he bore

"O Lord, grant compassion to that coquette
Give her appetite though I ail and fret

Let her be content with this drop of dew
The fruit of desire comes only from you

She never inquires of me anymore   1855
Since I stooped so low as to worship form

You are omniscient, I had no choice then
You are ever prior, I was nothing then

Accepting that sin is hard to accede
But how could it be considered cruelty?

Come, don't punish me for figures of speech
If metaphors were mixed in with my speech

I never intended her beside you
You other, and that moon other but you

While slave to the rapture of wheeling fate   1860
Could there have been in my words any weight?

Cast me down in chains, I've worshipped false gods
And drag me back to the service of God

Reap now my intentions all in desire
Unite me with the first of all desire

Let her whom I love clasp me to her breast
Milk and honey both in joy and distress

Set all right—alas, but this is absurd!
Ridiculous fantasy, false, absurd!

To ask the absurd from you is our right   1865
Desire's possibility is its right

I would never ask for passion to cease
Let severance end and that bliss increase

For those who love ease, desire is a trial
But pure delight for the masters of trial

Eternity's cup my senses will blur
Let union increase my longing for her

I'm sick with the grief of longing for pain
Of old I am well acquainted with pain

Let all my desire be colored the same   1870
Let this complaint be my constant refrain

Poetry, in the Form of a Nightingale, Gives Warning

While wandering weeping to no avail
He suddenly saw a drunk nightingale

The bird addressed Love, delivering this speech
That joined in one chain the links of his grief

"There's treasure inside this fortress concealed
Don't think the fort empty, fortune's found here

Set fire to it, let it float to the skies
Be master of that vast fortune inside

If you do not light this mansion ablaze   1875
You'll not find your love the rest of your days

That Chinese shah's daughter so full of ire
Will roast your heart like kebab on a fire

As long as this lofty vault is still here
No chance of escape will ever appear

Don't race around till your energy's spent
The lock on this gate is pure enchantment

That princess's mother was fairy-born
The girl's heart is set upon you alone

The quarrel between them is most severe   1880
For earth never can with fire be compeer

The fairies will turn against you in time
They'll drink your heart's blood like ruby-red wine

The wine in that garden where you caroused
Was all the pure blood of great padishahs

If you had not let your sword fall to her
She'd never have dared to take you prisoner"

183

When Love comprehended all of this well
He lit a great fire in that citadel

The raging fire set that whole church alight   1885
It's crucifixes sailed up to meet Christ

The images mounted up to the sky
Adorning these seven perches on high

And sending aloft once more his cold sigh
That brave soldier was kept safe from the fire

That fortress, the ground it stood on, all razed
The Chinese shah's daughter went up in flames

A magical treasure was disinterred
Wherein represented was all the world

But Beauty unique was not inside it   1890
And Love didn't stay to scrutinize it

He found both the Sword of Ah! on the ground
And prayer's arrow sent forth rising at dawn

That fairy-sprite boy then set out again
Relighting himself as fire does again

But what a road! Every step was a well
Each blade of grass was a serpent from hell

As thoughts of his loved one came to his mind
Each time he repeated words of this kind

"O moon, enough of injustice, come, now! 1895
Run, hear my plea for my plea has run out!"

Love's Emaciation

Love's weakness increased to such an extent
He could neither heave a sigh nor lament

He fell like a shadow from Sorrel Rose
A fiery spark disengaged from its coal

That moon of the world waned to a crescent
The sun of his glory turned in descent

The wine of his comeliness would not last
There was only one sip left in the glass

A weakness beyond the final degree 1900
Perhaps beyond even ceasing to be

A mere bubble on an ocean of pain
If he took a breath he'd burst with the pain

Without matter he was but a mere form
Significance rare without letter borne

The raiment of strength abandoned his skin
The silk of moonlight was too much for him

If only he opened up his bright wings
He'd reach the land of nonexistent things

A flame burning like a firefly by night   1905
He blinked off and on, now gone and now bright

The act of sight was a flood in his gaze
The light of his eye obstructed his way

He drowned in his weakness and misery
He thought his own color a bloody sea

He tangled up in the thread of his thought
He could not traverse the country of thought

The rays of his glance seemed crisscrossed by veins
That trapped him inside their fishnet-like strings

So weak that he froze, immobilized now   1910
He was like a flame that had been snuffed out

He'd be dispersed if he stirred in the air
He'd be lost in sound if he mumbled there

The bubbles in wine were cause of torment
He withered away at rose-perfume scent

No longer could he traverse month and year
The prospect of living had disappeared

Each instant while he traversed this life's range
His bodily parts became disarranged

Not parts, they were irreducible bits   1915
Beyond what imagination can split

Each hair dragged his body down like a chain
By them only could his form be maintained

You'd swear if you could look into his face
That aught and naught coincide in one place

Whoever has seen this will testify
Eternity in mortality lies

The Final Extent of Love's Wretchedness

Left there on the road his future was nil
He had neither strength to move nor be still

His heart by time's postures bloodied and   1920
   drowned
His vessel of health was turned upside-down

The goal so desired remained beyond reach
The trial of despair he'd ever repeat

His heart's glass had cracked in a hundred ways
He'd stopped still upon that bare, stony plain

Exhausted, amazed, too weak to draw breath
His body embraced the angel of death

He wearied at thought of life immortal
And merciless death seemed to him joyful

His heart cared for neither heaven nor hell 1925
Unmoved by mirth and by sadness as well

By waves of despair, fear and awe beset
He had no capacity for regret

There was no place in the world he could hide
There was nothing but death left he desired

But death meant all hope of union would cease
It wasn't the wine to cure his disease

He could not imagine what cure to seek
What road should he take without any feet

Fate's nectar had made him languid and slow 1930
He filled with resentment for friend and foe

Now Rivalry seemed sworn foe of his heart
No hope for his love would enter his heart

He had no hope left of reaching his lover
He did not expect to ever recover

In order to strengthen that hidden pain
He whispered this verse again and again

"My heart is consumed with exile, dear friend
Come now, for my heart is ruined, dear friend"

Poetry Arrives to the Rescue

The dawn of divine grace came as a sage   1935
Appeared on the road and lit up the way

But oh what a sage! The true dawn itself
His every word led to wisdom itself

The staff in his hand, the span of his gaze
Resplendent with light his angelic face

His countenance was the river of life
His hair was like moonlight perfectly white

His brow was the crescent moon of hope's feast
His every move brought the news of hope's peace

He spoke of the wisdom fate brought to bear   1940
His message conveyed from mankind's forebear

His white beard of Mansur's essence was made
His words of truth, trumpet of Judgment Day

In awe of that perfect mirror's degree
Aristotle lay his head on his knee

He lit Alexander's way like a flare
The sun and the moon ran after his trail

Like heaven he wore a rich robe of green
The spiritual Hizir carried his train

In him did the Sacred Spirit confide   1945
The cache of revelation at his side

His sparkling bright face, his hair purest white
Were like the sun's disk agleam in moonlight

He chanted the *seven verses* always
The second intellect studied his ways

He guarded abstractions of divine names
He gathered up scattered meanings arcane

That ray of the soul extolling God's praise
Came down like Koranic light to that place

He treated Love with all sympathy fit   1950
He captured his heart and made it a gift

"I am the physician famed of this age
Through all the land I am known as a sage

I've come with the remedy that you seek
If only you will accompany me

Since alchemy is the thing that you need
Since that is the cure of which you're in need

Don't wait, let's go to the Fort of the Heart
And there petition the Shah of the Heart

Traceless Beauty is that great sovereign's name   1955
By that title all the world knows her fame

It's she who commands the Fort of the Heart
She is the queen of the Land of the Heart

They brought her news of your infirmity
And so, ever wakeful, that shah sent me"

Love Regains Consciousness

He listened to these glad tidings and then
He died and was resurrected again

Glad tidings in which all goals coincide
A state of affairs beyond all defined

Bestowing the life immortal and more   1960
Glad tidings of all that he had longed for

All weakness was gone and now strength was here
Once heartsick, a glimpse of health now appeared

The heart's rose with one word had opened up
The hall of the mosque with one lamp lit up

The news of the alchemy within reach
And also the hope of Beauty unique

At all of this Love was stunned and confused
Now Rivalry was obscured from his view

O Saki, you are to Gabriel kin   1965
Fill my inspiration's cup to the brim

With life's trumpet blast arouse me afresh
Don't silence the Jesus of consciousness

O Saki be Israfil and give life
Exchange all our death for eternal life

The trumpet shall serve the wine at this feast
And resurrect the multitude of speech

O Saki, O Saki, it is not fit
The heroes of God are not separate

They call you the Sacred Spirit, Saki   1970
They say your words lead to intimacy

If it is with love that you have discourse
Who else but me can you be looking for?

Although there are many masters of speech
There's no one who has this spirit but me

I stopped speaking and the universe stilled
On Mount Sinai Moses left unfulfilled

Let the David of my heart compose Psalms
Leave gaping in awe the angels of song

Be generous, do, and give me good news   1975
This time make my taste of joy something new

Although all intoxications are one
All cry *"Yes,"* but *"Am I not your lord?"* one

Still since the lamp of love must never dim
Without me the axis of time won't spin

Bring me to my senses with one cup more
That I may be twice as drunk as before

It's all a stroll through the valley of cheer
God willing, it augers good fortune here

The sage took that youth with him down the road   1980
They went to the court in joy thousandfold

That joy which no words can ever explain
One laugh like that all the sky can't contain

The Heart's Fortress then emerged into view
And what did Love see?—behold now the view!

A fortress built all of red sapphire stone
A palace divine in this human home

Each brick was bejeweled with gold inlay spun
And sparkled there face-to-face with the sun

All images of invisible form   1985
Its towers and turrets mysteries of form

Multicolored lights from battlements streamed
The ramparts were treasures of mysteries

The spectacle such it dazzled the eyes
Words ran out—the place could not be described

One side of it faced a light-visaged sea
And one side a plain of billowing green

Five gates gazed out over that lucid sea
And five others did this earth oversee

Five gates, but they reached to God's throne
    on high   1990
Each tower as tall as Mount Kaf on high

There stood at each gate an angel supreme
Like spirit held dear and greatly esteemed

Their wings were the light of heaven azure
Like *Anka* birds on Kaf mountain so pure

Each one had his servants and retinue
With fairies like idols in multitudes

The five of the gates that looked on the sea
Were worthy of praise beyond all degree

Love looked at that city dumbstruck with awe   1995
Nor speaking nor silent, like as to naught

That sage said, "Do you not understand yet?
Have you not left your bedazzlement yet?

How long will bedazzlement be a trial?
The joy of bedazzlement is now nigh"

That boy like the moon recovered his wits
In one fell swoop passed the gloom of eclipse

In short, that perfected and pure sage soon
Arrived at the citadel with that moon

A city beyond all possible worlds   2000
The roads there were paved with eloquent pearls

The boulevards passed by rushing like streams
No one felt the need to walk with his feet

Love brimmed over drunkenly at the sight
While troops crowded round him all made of light

A white-mantled regiment came forth first
The envy of union's blissful sunburst

Alike to a flock of startling white deer
The sun dressed in morning's white robe of cheer

A thousand of them wore raiment of gold   2005
Gold-mantled, gold-turbaned, gold upon gold

Winged and houri-faced each and every one
From head to toe alchemy all of them

One regiment wore robes of deepest blue
They rose like an ocean in waves of blue

The golden among them faded from sight
Like stars shining faintly in the dark night

195

Another in red rushed forth to keep pace
Each holding paradise in fond embrace

As rivals of sun and moon forth they came   2010
Of heaven but flower beds of pure flame

A highly esteemed group came to be seen
By spirit possessed, all emerald green

A vast grassy sea, a regiment bright
Came rolling in waves of spiritual life

Another flank all in vestments of black
Like glittering stars inside dark night's wrap

Not one of them needs description or laud
Night, but the night of Muhammad's Miraj

In wave upon wave arrived those platoons   2015
In troop after troop with their hundred hues

Each regiment with its color unique
Was light in embodied form, so to speak

The various colors of their bright rays
Set fantasy's lights in warring display

But limpid and pure that fortress's floor
Was like the discerning intellect, mirror

With every reflection there were displayed
A thousand souls raised up for Judgment Day

Inside there were many mansions adorned   2020
With images like the Fortress of Forms

But here all the likenesses were alive
Not man-aping mandrakes of soul deprived

From out of each mansion's window there gazed
A thousand to rival China's fair maid

And then as those troops of light multihued
Came forward to pay Love their respects due

They offered themselves in service to him
They kissed his hand and swore service to him

At once there appeared a luminous throne   2025
Where Love and that wise sage sat down alone

Thus carrying that shah they set out in state
To tour through that city all on parade

The orchards and gardens on every side
Would bring shame upon Ridvan's paradise

Buried treasures there were open to view
Where stars shining bright were mixed in with jewels

So much unexplained by reason and chance
Was made clear to Love with each single glance

Recalling desire for Beauty to mind   2030
He looked out for Beauty's palace to find

When all of a sudden he saw her court
The wondrous pavilion of the shah's court

All of a piece emerald and chrysolite
Each window an immortal paradise

Hid by a thousand veils of the unseen
In doubt and in certainty unmoved, serene

That sage left his side descending the throne
And entered the court pavilion alone

Love waited there for an hour or two   2035
Until the sage came to bring him the news

When inside the court a clamor arose
Such as the age had never seen before

From *tamburs* and flutes exuberant strains
Like Judgment Day's trumpet, raucous refrains

The sounds of the drums of gaiety and joy
The signs of immortal gladness and joy

A curtain was suddenly lifted up
While Love was stunned and completely dumbstruck

Revealed there was an exceeding strange scene   2040
Of which Love could never ever have dreamed

Modesty, Dazzle, and Rivalry then
Came forward to offer service to him

And Poetry too that luminous sage
Together with Madness, sheikh of the age

And then Poetry announced the good news
He stepped forth and said, "Prince noble and true,

Do you understand this now, even you?
Who am I and where is this you've come to?

What heart-captivating city is this?   2045
What flourishing orchard garden is this?

What path is it you have traveled so long?
Your strength and skill came from which padishah?

Do you now remember the Sons of Love?
Meaning's Pleasure Place of union in love?

This place is that very same matchless grove
This mansion is yet that same fine abode

There are no ghouls here, no terrors, no fears
No black demon, no dread message of tears

No dark freezing winter, no magic fire   2050
No horror of death, no torment or trial

Here you will find only immortal joy
All kinds of delight, high spirits and joy

This mystery rare you now comprehend
Is veiled from the hearts of rational men

I am Poetry who came when you fell
And showed you how to escape from the well

It was I who slew the witch on your path
I cleared the way for you on every path

That eloquent parrot, that nightingale   2055
That sweet pheasant, all of them I as well

The sage and pure-natured physician too
I am the one who guided you all through

I've come now to tell you union awaits
See and understand the truth of this state

Of all these events there was but one cause
Your vision awry, therein lay the fault

For Love is but Beauty, and Beauty Love
You've practiced the path of error thereof

In unity there is no make-believe   2060
In that duty nothing that cannot be

Come now and behold that angelic face
See Beauty who has no peer and no price

That all once concealed may now be revealed
And all once revealed may now be concealed

Your friends of the path can come just so far
For only Love reaches that padishah

Not Rivalry, Modesty, or Madness
The Sons of Love, your tribe too must be left

And friendship with Poetry here has an end   2065
None but Dazzle may beyond this ascend"

And so Dazzle took that shah by the hand
The curtains of union parted at last

At this point the story comes to a close
What lies beyond this is not to be shown

Praised be God the living who does not die
Speech has to the realm of silence arrived

_____

I've outdistanced my predecessors' school
I've spoken a language with different rule

I did not conform to that company   2070
Who like Khusraw emulate Nizami

By God, this adventure is something else
Although it may be a tale of woe, yes

Do not assume this is just so-so style
Come on and try it yourself for a while

The masters of poetry all are well-known
Here is the pen, here the country of Rum

Have you seen this hidden valley before?
This ground's not the old Divan road of yore

Don't point an accusing finger like that 2075
Let's see you compose five more lines like that

It's true that I wrote it in a short while
But that is no sign my work's juvenile

There's many a *Shah and Slave* we have seen
Our fathers could have dashed off in their sleep

I found a new style in that buried vault
I opened that cache and I spent it all

I took its secrets from the *Masnavi*
I stole, but I stole common property

Endeavor to understand this yourself 2080
Find that precious pearl and steal it yourself

Don't grudge me this declaration of mine
Refer my soul on to favor divine

Of poethood now when no trace is felt
I am poetry's sultan—there's none else

O pen, this poetry is none of yours
O night, this break of day is none of yours

The teacher of Rum by light of his grace
Has made the horizons shine with my blaze

When I was a babe like half of a verse   2085
He made me stand up with poetry first

I was still a child too young to converse
And yet I grew full in fame with my verse

I had no schoolteacher, owe debt to none
He ordered my talent's work from page one

O God, O God, how generous and kind
Mature art of speech in an artless child

Grace came to me from our Master Rumi
I took instruction from the *Masnavi*

It was as if that sea boundless and vast   2090
Were like to the dyer's coloring vat

My heart *like the jackal* plunged in that sea
And all my companions crowded round me

I taunted the peacock of paradise
But I did not have the power of flight

I wailed like the flute, but all was for naught
No one but the candle wept at my song

A cauldron of wisdom filled up this breast
But fate chose the lips of others to bless

I rose up like the moon and I waxed full   2095
But in the end I was left void and null

My breast now will not with love or light shine
It was all a show for men of my time

Friends went into raptures at my success
Then went on their way reciting "God bless"

I'm left and those words on my lips are left
The ship of desire weighed anchor and left

My soul does not burn with will to aspire
Nor is my heart moved by joy of desire

Ah, woe is me, should I pass on like this   2100
May God grant the favor of his success

———————————

Galip, date this suffering's register thus
Its chronogram is *the seal thereof musk*

KEY

abdal   Blessed personages in charge of the world.

Abu Hanife   Founder of the Hanafi school of Islamic law, which the Ottomans followed. Galip refers to his ruling, which Abu Hanife later reversed, that in their prayers worshippers could recite Koranic verses in translation.

age of the moon   According to ancient lore, each of the seven planets, which included the moon, ruled for a thousand years. The prophet Muhammad lived in the age of the moon.

ahadiyet, Ahmediyet   Oneness, Ahmed-ness (Muhammad-ness). The Prophet's saying, "I am Ahmed without the letter *m*," is referred to here.

Aleppo silk   The silk of Aleppo was famous for its superior quality.

Alexander   According to legend, Alexander the Great had a mirror set up in the sea facing Alexandria. It showed ships coming from afar and lit them afire by reflecting the rays of the sun. He is mentioned with Hizir, because both sought the fountain of youth.

Ali   The Prophet's cousin and son-in-law, the fourth caliph, and the first Shiite imam, Ali is also known as the Lion. Galip's devotion to Ali signifies his Alevi sympathies (for certain Shiite principles) and was not, in his historical context, incompatible with Sunnite beliefs.

alif (ا), jeem (ج), ra (ر), meem (م), seen (س)   Arabic letters are likened here to things with similar shapes.

Anka   A huge, mythical bird that flies very high, sometimes identified with the phoenix.

Ashik Turani   If this is a real person, he is too obscure to be listed in the usual reference works. It may be a satirical name. An *ashik* is a folk minstrel; *Turani* means "of Turan," the legendary home of the Turks.

as it really is   See *Things as they really are.*

association   In couplet 815, the name of a common poetic device.

as things truly are   See *Things as they really are.*

Ayni   This is probably Ayni of Antep (1766–1838/39),* a very minor poet. He and Galip knew each other.

Azra   Legendary beloved of Vamik.

Azrail   The angel of death.

Badakhshan   A place in Iran known for ruby mines.

"Be!"   God creates with this command (Koran 2.117, 16.40, 36.82, 40.68).

Behzad   Legendary Persian miniature painter. Ferhad's father.

Betul   Nickname of both the Virgin Mary and the Prophet's daughter, Fatima.

Bilal   A freed African slave, one of the first Muslims, Bilal had a beautiful voice and served as the Prophet's muezzin (caller to prayer).

Bisutun   A mountain through which Ferhad opened a waterway, a task many before him had failed to perform.

black light   The most intense, spiritual light is called black light, the idea being that it can't be seen, that it makes the eyes go dark. It is thought that God has placed a speck of black light in every human heart.

boon universal   In couplet 1679, existence.

Broomsweep Softy, Tormented   If these are poets' proper names (Nermi Odabaşı) or pen names (Mihneti), they are not remembered well enough today to be listed in the usual reference works. They may be satirical names.

Burak   The Prophet's mount on the Miraj.

catapult   See *"Fire, be cold ..."*

chain mail of David   The prophet David is known as the inventor of chain-mail armor.

---

* A slash is used in dates to give the Gregorian approximation of an Islamic lunar year.

Chelebi   An honorific title used derisively in couplet 749.

David   The prophet David is known as the author of the Psalms.

death of red hue   One of the varieties of "voluntary death." The red death is achieved by resisting the lower impulses of the soul.

dispensation for awe   See *"We have not known you ..."* Galip also refers to the principle reiterated in the Koran (14.34, 16.18) that a human being cannot fully account for the favors of God.

Divan   A book of a poet's collected poems, and the Ottoman Imperial Council, and the name of a boulevard in Istanbul running by the Imperial Council chamber.

divine names   The divine names and attributes are the infinite qualities of God. The Truth is a divine name with a special status.

double blade of Ali   Ali's famous sword, Zulfikar, had a double blade.

Erguvan   A tree, sometimes called in English the Judas tree, but here having no Christian connotations. It quickly reproduces and blooms abundantly and repeatedly in early spring with very bright pink to red flowers, whose shedding petals carpet the ground.

Erjeng   A legendary book of paintings attributed to Mani, eponymous founder of Manicheanism.

Esat   Galip's given name. Galip was his pen name.

eternity   See *eternity in mortality.*

eternity in mortality   In this translation, "mortality" (*fena*) is a state in which the ego is annihilated in realization of unity with God, and "eternity" (*beka*) is the subsequent state of immortality in God.

Fahreddin   A jurist and professor active 1413–51.

Fahr-i Jurjan   Romance writer, also known as Gurgani (died 1050/51).

fantasy shade   A lampshade painted with scenes, which the heat of the flame causes to revolve, projecting the scenes on the surrounding surfaces.

Fatiha   The opening chapter of the Koran.

Ferdowsi   Author (died 1020) of the Persian Book of Kings.

Ferhad   Legendary lover who killed himself, misled to believe he had lost his beloved Shirin. He was a brilliant engineer and opened a waterway through Mount Bisutun.

"Fire, be cold ..."   Nimrod punished Abraham by throwing him by catapult into a fire, and God made the fire cold.

the first created ...   Reference to the Prophet's saying, "The first thing God created was my light."

first firmament   In the old Ptolemaic scheme, each planet inhabits a heavenly sphere enclosed by the one above it like the skins of an onion, with the earth at the center. The seven heavens are, in ascending order, that of the moon, Mercury, Venus, the sun, Mars, Jupiter, and Saturn. In Galip's Miraj chapter, the persons Muhammad encounters in each sphere are resident there according to ancient Middle Eastern lore.

five gates   In Rumi's *Masnavi*, it is the Fortress of Forms that has five gates facing the land and five facing the sea. Rumi explained that the five facing the land are the five senses, and those facing the sea, the inner faculties of apperception.

flax   Moonlight was thought to cause flax to rot (couplet 836).

Fortress of Forms   A castle of this name figures in the final story of Rumi's *Masnavi*, the story of the three princes.

Fuzuli   Poet, author (died 1555) of a famous Turkish version of the romance Leyla and Majnun.

Gazanfer   Lion, title of Ali.

God's Lion   Ali.

golden chain   In couplet 141, a chain of lineage leading back to the Prophet through Ali.

Harut   Harut and Marut (Koran 2.102) were angels sent down to Babel to test mankind. According to Middle Eastern lore, they met a tragic end when they fell in love with a woman, taught her God's greatest name in order to possess her, and were hung upside down in a well.

Hassan bin Sabit   A poet who lived in the time of the Prophet. The reason Galip has him ask forgiveness is that Hassan took a position against the caliphate of Ali.

Hayber   A fort conquered by Ali.

Hayder   Lion, title of Ali.

Hazret-i Hudavengar   Rumi.

heaven's judge   Jupiter.

heaven's vulture   Two small constellations in the northern sky.

he journeyed by night   Koran 17.1, referring to the Miraj.

Hizir   Immortal Hizir, variously considered a prophet or saint, is known for coming to the rescue of lost travelers. He is considered to be the one mentioned in the Koran (18.60–82) who taught Moses and who drank the water of life from the fountain of youth in the land of darkness, where he traveled with Alexander the Great.

hoopoe A bird that carried messages for King Solomon.

horse's belly I believe this is a reference to Rumi's *Masnavi* (6.3581), where it is a cow's belly; or it may be a reference to the Trojan horse. The idea is that, having already passed from one state of being to another, one should not regress.

Hulagu Known for his cruelty, a grandson of Genghis Khan.

Huma A huge, mythical bird with no feet, thought to bestow kingship to those on whom its shadow falls.

Ibn Adham A Muslim mystic (died circa 776–81) who like Buddha renounced his throne.

Ibn Melek A prominent jurist (died 1480/81).

Ibrahim Gulshani He died 1533/34. Wrote a parallel to Rumi's *Masnavi*.

Idris The prophet known for inventing writing and tailoring and for teaching astrology.

"If not for you...I would not have created the heavens." A sacred saying, in which God spoke to the prophet Muhammad.

Imad Famed scholar and historian (died 1211/12).

incomparability The incomparability of the Koran is proof of its divine origin.

Ismail Son of Abraham.

Israfil Raphael. He blows the trumpet on the Day of Judgment.

I will have good news In couplet 136, the idea is that one is forgiven only if one does wrong.

Jacob Father of the prophet Joseph, who so wept, mourning his son, that his eyes went white.

Jamshid, Jam A legendary Persian king who had a cup in which he could see all the world.

jinn Jinn (genies) are creatures made of fire. Satan is of their kind. They are sometimes thought to lurk around foul and dirty places.

Joseph The prophet, famed as the most beautiful man who ever lived.

the journey by night The Miraj.

jumped the sword   Sealed a vow.

juxtaposing   In couplet 811, a common poetic device.

Kaf mountain   A mythical mountain range thought to encircle the (flat) world.

Kaknus   A mythological bird with 365 nostrils that perches on mountains facing the wind, which produces sounds as it blows through the nostrils. Other birds, hearing these sounds, are attracted, and the Kaknus eats them. It lives for a thousand years, then gathers a pile of brush, sits on it, and flaps its wings. The flapping of its wings sets the brush on fire, and the bird burns up. An egg emerges from the ashes, and another Kaknus is born.

kanun   A kind of zither, played by striking the strings with wands. In couplet 1131 Beauty is likened to a musical instrument that is not being played.

Karun   An infamous miser whom God punished by causing the earth to swallow him up (Koran 28.81).

Kashmir   Known for its beautiful spring seasons and for the beautiful shawls made there.

Kay   Mythological Persian kings.

Kays   Majnun's given name.

Kerbala   The site of the martyrdom of Hussein, the Prophet's grandson.

Kevser   A river, or pool, in paradise.

Khusraw   Romance writer (died 1325) known as "the Parrot of India" and "God's Turk."

Khusrev   Persian king, legendary lover of Shirin.

Koran   In couplet 71, Muhammad is identified with the Koran.

Lahut   See *Nasut.*

lamp of night   A mythical gem that, because it generates light in itself, is often used as a symbol of the divine.

Lat   A pre-Islamic goddess worshipped in Arabia.

"Leave none without faith."   Noah's plea to God (Koran 71.26).

Leyla   The legendary beloved of Majnun.

like a pen   A reed pen's tip is slit down the middle (facilitating the flow of ink), thus "split-tongued."

like the jackal   In a proverbial story, told in Rumi's *Masnavi*, a jackal jumps into a dyer's vat hoping to resemble a peacock.

Magian belt   Worn by Zoroastrians.

Key

Majnun Litcrally "Mad," the legendary lover of Leyla.

Mani Eponymous founder of Manichaeanism, known for his beautiful paintings.

man of the eye Pupil of the eye.

Mansur al-Hallaj Muslim mystic (died 921) martyred for his famous statement, "I am the Truth."

Mary's palm When Mary was seized with labor pains, she clung to the trunk of a palm tree. A voice told her God had provided a stream running beneath the tree from which she could drink, and it told her to shake the tree and eat of the dates (Koran 19.23–26).

Masnavi Rumi's famed six-volume work of spiritual teachings in rhymed couplets.

medrese A seminary college.

Melekut, Jeberut Ontological levels situated between the highest planetary sphere and God's throne, Jeberut above Melekut, which is often identified with the realm of imagination.

mercy's book The Koran.

the Messiah In couplet 94, Jesus Christ.

Miraj Also called the Prophet's night journey or ascension, the Miraj was a mysterious journey taken on the miraculous mount Burak from Mecca to Jerusalem, where Muhammad led all the other prophets in prayer, then ascended the heavens to meet with God.

Mirza Jan Famed litterateur (died 1585/86).

Modaburnu A district of Istanbul on the Marmara.

Molla Religious teacher.

moon of Canaan The prophet Joseph.

moon of Nahsheb This legendary moon, reflected in a well although there is no moon in the sky, is a symbol of the self-subsistent divine.

mortality See *eternity in mortality.*

Mutazilite An eighth-ninth-century school of theology relevant here because it rejected the attribution of qualities to God, on which Galip's argument depends.

Nabi An Ottoman poet (died 1712) whose *Beneficity* is under discussion in Galip's chapter "The Reason for This Composition." As the most recent highly regarded romance in rhymed couplets, it was the work Galip would have to outdo.

Nahsheb See *moon of Nahsheb.*

211

naked   In couplet 382, *naked* means stripped of self, of ego.

name supreme   The *ism-i azam*, often said to be Allah, considered as the sum of all the divine names.

Nasut, Lahut   Ontological levels, Nasut that of humanity, Lahut that of the divine.

Nawfal   Tried unsuccessfully to convince Leyla's father to allow her marriage to Majnun.

Nefi   An Ottoman poet (died 1635) whose *Rahshiye* is a poem in praise of the horse Rahsh (mount of a hero from the Persian Book of Kings).

Nevai   Poet (died 1501) credited with founding the Turkish romance school.

Nevizade   Ottoman romance writer (died 1634).

night's lamp   See *lamp of night.*

Nimrod   Built the Tower of Babel. God punished him by having a mosquito enter his brain through his ear.

nine heavens   The number of heavenly spheres was thought of variously as nine or seven, as in the English expression "seventh heaven."

Nizami   A Persian poet (died 1209), founder of the romance tradition in rhymed couplets.

"None without faith"   See *"Leave none without faith."*

not-place, not-space   God is beyond place and time, so his location is referred to as not-place and his time as not-time.

owl   Owls are known to frequent ruins.

padishah, padshah   Alternative spellings of the title Shah of Shahs.

Perished be...   A chapter of the Koran (111) recited backward in order to obtain a desired result.

perpetual creation   The doctrine that God creates the world anew every instant, based on the Koran (50.15).

Plato's barrel   A traditional confusion with the barrel of Diogenes.

Ragib's *Writings*   The *Writings* of Ragib Pasha (died 1765), also a poet, were used as a guide to bureaucratic prose.

raki   An alcoholic drink identical to ouzo, which is clear and turns filmy white when mixed with water.

Refref   A flying carpet that, according to some accounts, the Prophet used on the Miraj.

the rending of his breast   Before the Miraj, Gabriel opened the
Prophet's breast, took out his heart, and bathed it in a golden
bowl full of faith.

Revani   This may be the poet Revani (died 1524), or an obscure
contemporary of Galip's, or a play on the word *revani,* which
means "easygoing."

Ridvan   A doorkeeper of paradise.

ruby ink   Red ink was used for headings in Ottoman books.

Rum   Rome, and the West in general.

Rustem   Hero of the Persian Book of Kings.

Sabit   An Ottoman poet (died 1712) of whom Galip had a low opin-
ion.

Sacred Spirit   The highest level of the spirit, variously identified,
often with the angel Gabriel.

saki   Cupbearer who serves wine at a gathering.

salamander   Salamanders are thought to thrive in fire.

Saturn   The planet is associated with the color black.

Scorpio   The position of the sun in Scorpio is considered unlucky,
as in couplet 337.

"the seal thereof musk"   Koran 83.26. In paradise the righteous
will slake their thirst on a pure wine whose seal will be of musk.
The Arabic letters of the Koranic phrase are equal to 1197, the
Islamic lunar year in which Galip finished his work.

seven verses   The opening chapter of the Koran.

Seyyid   Here, the prophet Muhammad.

Shah and Slave   A story that was the subject of many tales and
romances.

Shams of Tabriz   A man who was a special inspiration to Rumi.

Shapur   A friend of Ferhad who carried letters between him and
Shirin.

Shavkat   A Persian poet (died 1695/96) of the Indian style, known
for complex imagery, of which Galip is considered the greatest
Ottoman master.

Shebdiz   Khusrev's horse.

Sheikh Attar   A Persian poet (died 1220). In couplets 186–87, Galip
asserts that Nabi took the plot of *Beneficity* from Attar's *Book of
Divinity.*

Sheikh of Islam   Highest functionary in the Ottoman religious establishment.

Shirin   Legendary beloved of both Khusrev and Ferhad.

"Show yourself to me."   What Moses asked God, and God replied "You shall not see me ..." (Koran 7.143).

Siddiq   Usually a title of Abu Bakr, the first caliph, leader of the Islamic community after the Prophet's death; but it can also refer to Ali.

the Sidre tree   The tree beyond which Gabriel was unable to go with the Prophet during the Miraj.

Sineçak   An Ottoman mystic who compiled a famous selection from Rumi's *Masnavi*.

sites manifest   Sites of manifestation are places—things and persons—manifesting divine names and attributes.

the space of two bows...or nearer   Koran 53.9, here interpreted as how close the Prophet came to God on the Miraj and expressed as two bows, as in bows and arrows, standing on end and touching so as to form a circle of unity.

split in two   One of the Prophet's miracles was his splitting of the moon (Koran 54.1–3).

story of many branches   A proverbial tale about a man who lost his camel, mentioned when someone tells a long, pointless story.

stream of milk   When Shirin wanted milk, Ferhad arranged to have it flow to her in a canal he dug to her palace through Mount Bisutun.

Sufi   In English the term has come to mean a practitioner of Sufism, Islamic mysticism, and a member of a dervish order, a *tarikat*. But in Ottoman Turkish the word *sofu* meant "seminary student" and had a strong connotation of complacent (and sometimes pretentiously meddlesome, or even violently reactionary) immaturity in religious understanding.

Suha   A very small star.

Sumenat   A Hindu temple in Gujarat adorned with many statues.

Summary   A manual of rhetoric.

Surhab   A mountain near Tabriz, red in color, having no vegetation or water.

Sütlüce   A district of Istanbul on the Golden Horn, where Galip lived.

Tablet, Pen   The Tablet is mentioned in the Koran 85.22. The Pen is treated in a number of hadith.

tambur   A long-necked lute.

Tesnim   A spring in paradise.

things as they really are   Reference to the Prophet's saying, "O God, show me every thing as it really is."

thirtieth of the Koran   The Koran is divided into thirty parts for memorization and recital.

thus proposed God   When people accused the prophet Muhammad of composing the Koran himself, they were challenged to compose something like it (Koran 2.24, 10.39, 11.14, 17.89).

to guide aright   Reference to a debate of early Muslim theology over predestination and free will, focusing on whether or not God is obliged to guide man aright.

the Tuba tree   A huge tree in paradise.

Ukaz   A village near Mecca where an annual poetry competition was held in pre-Islamic times, the winning verses being hung up in the Kaaba.

Ummehani   Sister of Ali. Muhammad was an overnight guest in her home on the night of the Miraj.

unseen   In couplet 436, a reference to the Koran (2.3).

Vamik   Legendary lover of Azra.

the verse of light   A very famous verse of the Koran (24.35), in which God is likened to light.

Veys el-Qarani   He became a Muslim in the time of the Prophet without having met the Prophet. He serves as an example of someone who achieves guidance without a guide.

"We have not known you ..."   A saying of the Prophet's, referring to God. It was the subject of a conversation between Rumi and Shams of Tabriz, on their first meeting. Shams asked how the Prophet could have said that, and Rumi answered that it was because the Prophet's desire for knowledge of God was infinite. This saying is often cited in support of the principle that human spiritual poverty is the perfect, inverse complement of divine plenitude.

white hands   One of Moses's miracles was the transfiguration of his hand with pure white light (Koran 7.108, 20.22, 27.12, 28.32).

"will not fail ..." A reference to the sacred saying, in which God spoke to the prophet Muhammad: "My servant does not fail to approach me through acts of (supererogatory) worship until I love him, and when I love him, I become the hearing by which he hears, the seeing by which he sees, and the tongue by which he speaks."

with a finger traced An expression meaning that something is so obvious, you can point to it with a finger.

without doubt In couplets 436 and 706, a reference to the Koran (2.2).

"Yes," but "Am I not your Lord?" According to the Koran (7.172), before creating the world, God gathered all the souls of mankind and asked them this question, and they answered yes.

"You shall not see me." See *"Show yourself to me."*

youth sworn to serve Followers of *futuwwah*, a medieval code of chivalry.

Zal Father of Rustem, hero of the Persian Book of Kings. Zal was born with white hair, and his name is synonymous with old age.

Zamzam A well near Mecca, which Abraham dug for his son Ismail. According to legend, Ismail wept in thirst, and this spring bubbled up under his feet.

Zuhre, Zehra Zuhre is a name of Venus. Zehra was a nickname of the Prophet's daughter, Fatima. In couplet 92, the similarity of their names serves as a fanciful cause (a common poetic device) for the Prophet's pardon of Venus.

Zuleyha Loved the prophet Joseph and in her attempt to seduce him locked him in a room painted with erotic pictures of herself.

Zulfikar Ali's double-bladed sword.

Modern Language Association of America
Texts and Translations

To purchase MLA publications,
visit www.mla.org/bookstore

Texts

Anna Banti. *"La signorina" e altri racconti.* Ed. and introd. Carol Lazzaro-Weis. 2001.

Bekenntnisse einer Giftmischerin, von ihr selbst geschrieben. Ed. and introd. Raleigh Whitinger and Diana Spokiene. 2009.

Adolphe Belot. *Mademoiselle Giraud, ma femme.* Ed and introd. Christopher Rivers. 2002.

Dovid Bergelson. אָפּגאַנג. Ed. and introd. Joseph Sherman. 1999.

Elsa Bernstein. *Dämmerung: Schauspiel in fünf Akten.* Ed. and introd. Susanne Kord. 2003.

Edith Bruck. *Lettera alla madre.* Ed. and introd. Gabriella Romani. 2006.

Mikhail Bulgakov. Дон Кихот. Ed. Margarita Marinova and Scott Pollard. 2014.

Isabelle de Charrière. *Lettres de Mistriss Henley publiées par son amie.* Ed. Joan Hinde Stewart and Philip Stewart. 1993.

Isabelle de Charrière. *Trois femmes: Nouvelle de l'Abbé de la Tour.* Ed. and introd. Emma Rooksby. 2007.

François-Timoléon de Choisy, Marie-Jeanne L'Héritier, and Charles Perrault. *Histoire de la Marquise-Marquis de Banneville.* Ed. Joan DeJean. 2004.

Sophie Cottin. *Claire d'Albe.* Ed. and introd. Margaret Cohen. 2002.

Marceline Desbordes-Valmore. *Sarah.* Ed. Deborah Jenson and Doris Y. Kaddish. 2008.

Claire de Duras. *Ourika.* Ed. Joan DeJean. Introd. DeJean and Margaret Waller. 1994.

Şeyh Galip. *Hüsn ü Aşk.* Ed. and introd. Victoria Rowe Holbrook. 2005.

Françoise de Graffigny. *Lettres d'une Péruvienne.* Introd. Joan DeJean and Nancy K. Miller. 1993.

Sofya Kovalevskaya. Нигилистка. Ed. and introd. Natasha Kolchevska. 2001.

Thérèse Kuoh-Moukoury. *Rencontres essentielles.* Introd. Cheryl Toman. 2002.

Juan José Millás. *"Trastornos de carácter" y otros cuentos.* Introd. Pepa Anastasio. 2007.

Emilia Pardo Bazán. *"El encaje roto" y otros cuentos.* Ed. and introd. Joyce Tolliver. 1996.

Rachilde. *Monsieur Vénus: Roman matérialiste.* Ed. and introd. Melanie Hawthorne and Liz Constable. 2004.

Marie Riccoboni. *Histoire d'Ernestine.* Ed. Joan Hinde Stewart and Philip Stewart. 1998.

George Sand. *Gabriel.* Ed. Kathleen Robin Hart. 2010.

Eleonore Thon. *Adelheit von Rastenberg.* Ed. and introd. Karin A. Wurst. 1996.

Translations

Anna Banti. *"The Signorina" and Other Stories.* Trans. Martha King and Carol Lazzaro-Weis. 2001.

Adolphe Belot. *Mademoiselle Giraud, My Wife.* Trans. Christopher Rivers. 2002.

Dovid Bergelson. *Descent.* Trans. Joseph Sherman. 1999.

Elsa Bernstein. *Twilight: A Drama in Five Acts.* Trans. Susanne Kord. 2003.

Edith Bruck. *Letter to My Mother.* Trans. Brenda Webster with Gabriella Romani. 2006.

Mikhail Bulgakov. *Don Quixote.* Trans. Margarita Marinova. 2014.

Isabelle de Charrière. *Letters of Mistress Henley Published by Her Friend.* Trans. Philip Stewart and Jean Vaché. 1993.

Isabelle de Charrière. *Three Women: A Novel by the Abbé de la Tour.* Trans. Emma Rooksby. 2007.

François-Timoléon de Choisy, Marie-Jeanne L'Héritier, and Charles Perrault. *The Story of the Marquise-Marquis de Banneville.* Trans. Steven Rendall. 2004.

Confessions of a Poisoner, Written by Herself. Trans. Raleigh Witinger and Diane Spokiene. 2009.

Sophie Cottin. *Claire d'Albe.* Trans. Margaret Cohen. 2002.

Marceline Desbordes-Valmore. *Sarah.* Trans. Deborah Jenson and Doris Y. Kaddish. 2008.

Claire de Duras. *Ourika.* Trans. John Fowles. 1994.

Şeyh Galip. *Beauty and Love.* Trans. Victoria Rowe Holbrook. 2005.

Françoise de Graffigny. *Letters from a Peruvian Woman.* Trans. David Kornacker. 1993.

Sofya Kovalevskaya. *Nihilist Girl.* Trans. Natasha Kolchevska with Mary Zirin. 2001.

Thérèse Kuoh-Moukoury. *Essential Encounters*. Trans. Cheryl Toman. 2002.

Juan José Millás. *"Personality Disorders" and Other Stories*. Trans. Gregory B. Kaplan. 2007.

Emilia Pardo Bazán. *"Torn Lace" and Other Stories*. Trans. María Cristina Urruela. 1996.

Rachilde. *Monsieur Vénus: A Materialist Novel*. Trans. Melanie Hawthorne. 2004.

Marie Riccoboni. *The Story of Ernestine*. Trans. Joan Hinde Stewart and Philip Stewart. 1998.

George Sand. *Gabriel*. Trans. Kathleen Robin Hart and Paul Fenouillet. 2010.

Eleonore Thon. *Adelheit von Rastenberg*. Trans. George F. Peters. 1996.

Texts and Translations in One Volume Anthologies

Modern Italian Poetry. Ed. and trans. Ned Condini. Introd. Dana Renga. 2009.

Modern Urdu Poetry. Ed., introd., and trans. M. A. R. Habib. 2003.

Nineteenth-Century Women's Poetry from France. Ed. Gretchen Schultz. Trans. Anne Atik, Michael Bishop, Mary Ann Caws, Melanie Hawthorne, Rosemary Lloyd, J. S. A. Lowe, Laurence Porter, Christopher Rivers, Schultz, Patricia Terry, and Rosanna Warren. 2008.

Nineteenth-Century Women's Poetry from Spain. Ed. Anna-Marie Aldaz. Introd. Susan Kirkpatrick. Trans. Aldaz and W. Robert Walker. 2008.

Spanish American Modernismo. Ed. Kelly Washbourne. Trans. Washbourne with Sergio Waisman. 2007.